THE INVISIBLE ENEMY

THE
INVISIBLE ENEMY

BY
GEORGE C. SHEDD
Author of "The Lady of Mystery House,"
"The Princess of Forge," etc

CONTENTS

THE INVISIBLE ENEMY

THE INVISIBLE ENEMY

I

SEVERAL GENTLEMEN WHO COVET A SHIPYARD

LOCAL CAPITAL supposed it had appraised all of Martinsport's possibilities, winnowed the profitable from the profitless, collected such assets as were worth while, present and future, and carefully tucked them away in its bosom. The term Local Capital may mean various things according to its location, mass, cohesion, specific gravity, and morality. In Martinsport it signified a select number of affluent citizens (more particularly, five) who had buttoned up in their breast-pockets everything of value in town, as aforesaid, for personal benefit rather than public weal, in contradistinction to affluent gentlemen from elsewhere who desired the same monopoly. The difference was clear and important. While the former were Local Capital, the latter were merely "outside money." Having as it believed everything of value safely buttoned up, Local Capital smiled when "outside money" came nosing about—until Stokes Brothers arrived.

Martinsport was a prosperous little city. It had a dredged channel out to deep water and a thriving export trade; it had an east-and-west main line railway that made it the center of the immediate coast, and two other lines that came down from the interior to tide-water. The latter roads discharged here immense quantities of turpentine, staves, lumber, cotton, molasses and so on, which vessels with neutral colors painted fore and aft upon their hulls and vessels with plain hulls but flying flags of the Allies stowed in their hulls, then sailed away again out into the Gulf of Mexico, keeping a sharp lookout for whales that wore periscopes on their backs.

From the water-front two long piers projected into the sea, where ships lay end to end, their masts penciled against the sky, taking on freight. Some distance east of them, amid heaps of oyster shell, there smoked a row of canneries. Westward, the water-front was occupied by boat-sheds and fishhouses for a mile or more, when they yielded to a broad shell drive bordered by white mansions.

The basin formed by the two piers had, like the channel, been dredged and therefore held deep water. A strip of ground that overlooked this harbor and in a sense connected the two piers remained vacant until along in the fall of 1916. The property was owned by an elderly gentleman, who had acquired it at the time the piers were built and allowed it to lie idle. Strictly speaking, the owner, a Mr. Willard, was "outside money" as his interests were elsewhere; lumber companies up in the state, timber tracts on the Pacific coast, and holdings in a trust company in Detroit, in a steel concern in Birmingham, a smelter in Arizona, a sugar refinery in New Orleans, and in a few other things. But as he spent his winters in Martinsport and no longer engaged actively in business and it was further known he had no designs upon Martinsport, he was regarded with an amiable eye. Financially he swam, when he did swim, in other and larger waters than those to which Local Capital was accustomed.

One or another of the capitalists of Martinsport had sought at various times to acquire this piece of property. It was not considered one of the things absolutely necessary to have and button up, as it appeared to have no especial value aside from its nearness to the piers, but it might possess speculative possibilities. However, the price asked by its owner, Mr. Willard, struck the prospective purchasers as ridiculously high, and so no deal had been made. When Local Capital bought, it bought only at a bargain; when it sold—but, ah, that was another matter!

The strip of ground remained vacant, as previously remarked, until in the autumn of 1916. All at once it became known that the property had been sold to a firm of the name of Stokes Brothers. Railroad trackage went down on it, a high board fence went up around it, and a swarm of workmen fell to work on ship ways. Inquiry confirmed the fact that Stokes Brothers proposed to build ships, wooden ships, ocean-going sailing ships. While every one knew that the war had given the ship-building business an unprecedented boom, kiting ship prices to unheard-of figures, no one had ever thought of the industry as a profitable possibility for Martinsport. The oyster-canning companies built a number of their little schooners here, to be sure, but they were a side-issue. And yet, with lumber dumped down at the port at a low freight cost, why should it not be a good business, ship-building? Then "just look at what ships were bringing!" Indeed, Local Capital began hurriedly to look at what ships were bringing. If Martinsport had a good thing like that, then rightfully Local Capital should profit by it instead of outside money. It looked hurriedly, but at no great length, for brief consideration disclosed that the only water-frontage on water deep enough to launch an ocean vessel lay between the two piers, leaving out the fact it had all the other facilities—Stokes Brothers' ground. Local Capital felt that somehow it had been hoodwinked, betrayed, robbed by misrepresentation. Mr. Willard, the former owner, came in for some rather bitter comment—but not to his face.

The matter was privately discussed in the board room of the Electric Light and Power Company, after a meeting of the directors whereat various petitions for lower light rates and six-for-a-quarter car fares and other confiscatory measures were summarily tossed into the paper basket. Local Capital constituted the board of directors.

"If Willard knew when he sold it what the tract was to be used for, and first did not give us a chance, then I say he deliberately affronted us." And the speaker, Johnson by name, president of the Marine Exchange National Bank, a gentleman plump of face and pompous of nature, looked around the table with a contenance pink with indignation. "What do you think, Farrington?"

"Yes, he played it pretty low, when he knew any one of us would have bought the ground—when several of us had tried to buy it, in fact."

Samuel Farrington was a shriveled little man, with a white chin whisker and hands whose natural position was a clutch. He always dressed in black. Though not an officer of the Martinsport Lumber and Cotton Bank, a rival financial institution of that of Johnson's, he nevertheless owned it body and soul.

There were three or four other banks in the town, but they did not count beside Johnson's and Farrington's. In the councils of the Big Five, as Local Capital was sometimes called, the two gentlemen, naturally conservative by disposition, aligned themselves together against the bolder element, namely, Derland, head of the light-and-power company and Main, of the gas concern—known as "Gas" Main. A cleavage of opinion usually existed as to ways and means between the bank pair on the one hand and the public utilities on the other. A third and distinct factor at the board was Mr. James Broussard, of whom more presently. Suffice it to say, the fifth member of Local Capital played a lone hand and formed no permanent alliances.

"I feel that Martinsport should have had this opportunity at ship-building, on the principle of home benefits accruing to home interests that have created the opportunity," Johnson continued, swelling a bit at the resonance of his own voice.

Derland, a small dark man, wearing a thin black mustache, removed his cigar and eyed Johnson across the table.

"All very true, but that doesn't help matters unless you've some suggestion as to how we're to have some of the benefits," he remarked, in level tones. "It's not a question of Willard any longer, but of Stokes Brothers."

"I've no suggestion, except that we pool together and buy them out," was the reply.

"But only at the figure of their investment; we'll pay these outsiders no fancy bonus," Farrington interjected, sharply.

"You're a fool if you think they'd be that easy," Main shot at the other, bluntly. "Of course, we'd have to make it an object to them to sell."

He lay back in his chair and began to meditate the idea. His figure was of large bulk, but not fat. His gray eyes had a hard steely light that seldom faded, while under his heavy brown mustache his mouth gripped a cigar in an unvarying, powerful trap-hold. Not many people addressed him directly as "Gas" Main.

"Any one know anything of these Stokes?" Derland asked.

"From somewhere west, I understand," Johnson stated.

"Pacific coast—Seattle," Farrington announced. "The firm opened a small account at my bank."

Johnson, of the other institution, having his attention thus called to the matter, made a mental note to dispatch the assistant-cashier to interview Stokes Brothers regarding starting an account with the Marine Exchange also. Farrington should not have that all to himself.

"Presuming that the new company would not sell outright, there's a possibility of it disposing of some of its stock to us," Derland said.

"Yes—and we might eventually secure control of the business, once we were in it," Johnson added, with a nod. "Local interests should control local enterprises."

"I'll talk with him next time he's in the bank," Farrington said, pinching the end of his nose.

"Gas" Main lowered his eyes until they rested on those of the little weazened speaker.

"And remember you're talking for all of us when you do," he said, in an inimical tone. "I don't trust you; you're nearly as bad as Broussard. Don't think you can pocket for yourself whatever stock they will sell. I'll make you eat your own whiskers if you try to double-cross me."

Farrington gave the man an angry glance, then pretended to ignore him.

"How many brothers are there in the firm?" Derland inquired.

"Only one in Martinsport—Frederic W. Stokes. Young, about thirty-six. He says he'll run the work here," Farrington said, shortly and with an involuntary scowl at Main. "That's all our bank got out of him. There may be twenty brothers at home."

Main continued to stare at Farrington.

"You've been trying to pump him, I see," he remarked, emitting a slow puff of smoke. "I wouldn't be surprised if you'd been cooking up a little scheme by yourself to grab off stock—that is, you and Johnson—and leave the rest of us out in the cold."

"I've never said a word to him on the subject!" the other exclaimed, in a rage. "Haven't more than seen the man, let alone talking to him."

"That doesn't say you haven't been scheming something. But don't you try it. If there's to be any pickings out of this ship business, we all share. You don't work a squeeze alone, remember that. Eh, Derland?"

"Right. We'll all participate," the second public utility replied, in a calm voice.

It will be observed that while Local Capital was banded together in a united cause against outside money, its members were not averse to putting a hand in each other's pockets when opportunity arose.

Johnson here endeavored to pour oil upon the conversation that threatened to grow acerbous.

"If we could once get an interest in this concern, then undoubtedly there would be ways of convincing Stokes Brothers it would be to their advantage to dispose to us of all their holdings in the business. Let us not dispute; there would be enough for all of us in that case. Unless they are a company of very large capital——"

"I looked them up. No ship-building firm of that name any place I could learn of," Farrington interrupted. "So it must be new."

"So much the better for us," said Main.

"Is Willard backing it?" Derland inquired.

"No. I had Ginn call him up saying he was preparing an article for the *Herald* about the new firm —which Ginn is—and that he heard Willard had an interest in it. Willard said he had not." Farrington still showed a trace of asperity in his words.

"Well, next time you see Stokes bring up the matter of a purchase of stock," Main said, coolly, "representing that there's a small local syndicate which would be pleased to invest. That is, unless some of you aren't interested, in which case I'll take your share." And he gazed about.

No one showed such a disposition. The ship industry had every appearance of traveling high and far in the next few years.

"First, sound him as to a sale outright," Derland appended.

"We could afford to pay above par for a controlling share of the stock," Johnson mused.

"What's the amount of the company's capital?"

Farrington shook his head, "Haven't learned. But it doesn't have to be large; two or three hundred thousand would be enough to launch the business." He began to rub his hands softly. "It's the earnings that count, ah, the earnings! They'll be something to admire, gentlemen. Once the company is going full capacity, it will earn the amount of its capital every six months. I can't see—no, I can't see how we were so blind as to let these strangers come in here and pick up the only available site for a shipyard from under our noses! Willard deceived us."

"We'll have to make it up from Stokes Brothers, that's all," Johnson stated, with an air that plainly indicated the matter was settled.

At this juncture in the proceedings, Mr. James Broussard laughed a low laugh, a derisive laugh. A low and derisive laugh was exactly what might have been expected from him, for his dark, thin, saturnine face at the moment was also derisive. He was a tall spare gentleman, but in no way weak; though leisurely of movement, he could on occasion be exceedingly agile. Of about the age of fifty-five, he wore a closely-trimmed brown Vandyke beard showing streaks of gray and had black eyes so full as to be almost insolent. Broussard was not the president of anything, but nevertheless a director in everything in Martinsport. He was a part of Local Capital, because Local Capital couldn't help itself. At one time Broussard money was about all there was to Local Capital; that was before there was a Martinsport.

Neither the bankers nor the pair of public utilities could claim Jim Broussard. He sat between them, as it were, and kept both uneasy. His four confrères viewed him with perpetual suspicion; he viewed them with amusement. If four honorable burglars were forced constantly to associate with an assassin of independent mind and faithless nature, they would have felt the arrangement no more distasteful than did the rest of Local Capital. He had no more conscience about breaking a gentleman's agreement with them when finally entered into than he had of skinning an enemy. Worse, he did not mind bleeding a little himself if only they bled more. That was against all the ethics! One can never feel entirely comfortable with a companion who uses a knife for pleasure as well as business.

As remarked, Broussard laughed at Johnson's statement. Offering no views or suggestions during the discussion, though occasionally glanced at as if invited for an opinion, the malice in his laughter was not unsignificant.

"Well, what strikes you as funny, Broussard?" Johnson demanded, loudly.

"Your air of proprietorship, to be sure. Already in your mind you've turned Stokes Brothers out into the cold, cold world and have their ship business in your pockets. It's as good as a French farce to hear you fellows quarreling about something you haven't got—and are not going to have. I'll give you some news. Stokes Brothers' business isn't for sale; they will keep right on making ships at their own convenience. Nor is any of their stock for sale. In respect to that, I may say that I've conferred with Mr. Frederic Stokes regarding the matter, and my most agreeable offers were declined without the least show of heart. Alas, gentlemen, I grieve to say it, but apparently he fails to appreciate the prestige his business would receive by the addition of Martinsport capital." And, removing his cigarette, he smiled his diabolical smile.

"Trust you to try and grab the stock for yourself," Farrington snapped, clawing his white chin whisker.

"Oh, I keep stepping along."

"Gas" Main tossed his cigar into a brass cuspidor.

"You're such a liar, Jim, I don't believe you ever saw the man at all," said he.

Broussard greeted this polite impeachment by an airy wave of his hand.

"Then help yourself to stock," he replied.

"Possibly some of the rest of us would impress Mr. Stokes—ahem—more favorably in presenting Martinsport's claims," said Johnson, placing the tips of his fingers together and gazing judicially down his nose. "I'll undertake to put matters to him in such a light that he'll perceive the mutual ad-

vantages and benefits to result from coöperation
of——"

"Go to it, brethren," Broussard interrupted, aris-
ing from his seat. "May hope be a candle to light
your way! He expects you fellows, I imagine, for
I told him you'd all probably be along one after
another, as you could smell easy money farther than
anybody I knew. Of course, if I couldn't finger
any of it, I hoped you gentlemen would likewise
refrain from a sense of delicacy. But to make sure,
I blackened your characters until he undoubtedly
thought you a gang of scoundrels somehow left un-
hanged. And he thanked me for the warning.
'Watch 'em,' I said, 'watch 'em now and hereafter.
And lock up your safe when they're about.' He
was locking it as I went out."

"I don't put such infamy past you," Johnson exclaimed in a burst of wrath at this disclosure, leaping to his feet and shaking a finger at Broussard.

Derland motioned him back into his seat.

"Don't let him make a goat of you," he remarked.
"He simply says that to see you squirm: haven't
you learned that yet?"

"Goat or no goat, it's outrageous! I'll see Stokes
anyway—and I'll say here and now that if we persuade him to part with some stock, Broussard will
get none of it!"

The latter lifted his walking-stick in a pained
gesture.

"Now, now, Johnson. You can count me out of
the spoils, but I pray you spare my sensibilities. Mr.

Stokes made it plain that I couldn't buy into the company, so I wash my hands of the matter and give my thoughts to higher things than mere sordid money-getting. But don't be so unkind as to tell me to my face, Johnson, that I can't share your own good luck; that is brutal."

He sauntered towards the door.

"A good thing, then, you don't hear what people say behind your back," Farrington whipped out.

"Nothing about foreclosing mortgages on poor widows, at any rate," Broussard returned with a meaningful smile as he paused, hand on the knob. "By the way, any of you fellows like to go over to New Orleans with me this afternoon and count the chickens? Ah, you sly dogs! I know all about your little private business trips—little suppers, wine, pretty girls. Don't scowl, Farrington, you old scamp, I've mentioned no names. Thank God, I'm an honest man and above board!"

Farrington sputtered and clawed the papers on the table before him, impotently.

"You damned devil, I'm a deacon of a church —I've not been in New Orleans in a year!" he squealed.

The closing door cut off Broussard's laughter.

II

A PLAN OF ACTION

To the chagrin of Johnson, after making the acquaintance of Frederic Stokes, of Stokes Brothers, and arranging a meeting with him, the prediction made by Broussard unhappily proved true. No stock of the ship-building company was for sale. The banker's most adroit persuasion and most plausible arguments failed to impress the other that the firm would materially benefit by admitting Local Capital into the concern. The ship-builder intimated that Stokes Brothers had a good thing and intended to keep it. When the company needed money, as later on might be the case, he would be glad to give Johnson's bank a chance at the loan; but no stock was being offered. He would consider Martinsport's interests to that extent, no further.

"It's a question whether the Marine Exchange or any other bank in town would care to make you a loan," Johnson remarked, with abruptness, "if no local capital is invested in the company."

"Then your loans are not determined by the character of the security alone, as is generally the banking practice?"

"Certainly—but every bank gives preference to

customers with home interests. Yours is an outside business, strictly speaking, Mr. Stokes."

A faint smile showed on the visitor's lips.

"How do you make that out?" he asked. "The investment is here. It provides a pay-roll for Martinsport. Except for material, our money is spent here."

"Very true. Yet no local money is in the business. Our town is benefited only incidentally and in the larger sense has nothing added to its wealth, so long as the industry is owned entirely outside."

Stokes dropped his smile, looked at his watch. From his face the banker, who had furtively observed it during the talk, had gathered nothing. The ship-builder appeared quite calm, indeed, casual.

"Well, that's a rather more narrow view of the matter than is taken out in the country where I come from," Stokes said. "Cities invite new industries there, and banks finance them. But it's unimportant in any case. I threw out the suggestion of your banks handling our loans, if we make them, in line with your argument of giving business to Martinsport. But if your institutions are hostile to outside enterprises, as you call them, why, we need not discuss the matter. It's of no concern to us. We had counted on floating our loans in Seattle anyway, where they look good to the bankers. We'll not trouble you, rest assured. And I'm pleased to be enlightened as to Martinsport's attitude towards our company; I'll bear it in mind in the future when it comes to hiring labor and buying such supplies as I've purchased here in the past. I'll begin replacing my carpenters at once with men from New Orleans. I can run up a boarding-house and commissary in the shipyard in no time. You'll have no objection, I presume, to my quoting your view of our company in explanation of my discontinuing purchases from local jobbing houses?"

Again the visitor consulted his watch, then arose from his chair. His manner was that of one who considered the present subject disposed of and who had other affairs to attend to.

The president of the Marine Exchange also got hastily to his feet. His round, pink face was a picture of agitated feelings, of consternation. It was the usual thing for men coming into his private office to be subdued if not abashed by a sense of his importance and that of the bank; but Stokes had not only not been awed but under Johnson's attempted pressure had produced a bomb that threatened to explode with unpleasant results.

"Wait a moment, Mr. Stokes," he exclaimed. "You misunderstood my words. There's no such feeling of hostility towards your company by me or my bank as you seem to think—not in the least, sir, not in the least. We welcome any worthy industry to Martinsport, like yours. I had no idea whatever of depreciating the benefits the town receives from your investment, let me make that clear to you. Sit down, Mr. Stokes, sit down and we'll talk it over. You mustn't depart with a wrong conception of our sentiments and business purposes. I greatly regret that I expressed myself so obscurely on the matter."

"I'm afraid I must return to the yard; my time is limited," was the answer.

"Now, now, Stokes, the ships won't float away. I want to set myself right in your opinion." Johnson smiled amiably and laid a hand upon the visitor's arm. "You mustn't think for an instant that I sought to discourage you——"

"Stokes Brothers is not discouraged that easily."

"I judge not—a live, enterprising company. I'm greatly interested in it, want to see it succeed. You must get the notion out of your head that we here in Martinsport are inimical to your firm. I can't satisfy you on that point better than by saying come to us when you want a loan. When you've become better acquainted with us, you'll see we're quite as obliging as the banks with whom you've been in the habit of dealing."

"I'll think it over. There will be no condition of selling stock if I do."

"Certainly not; it will be a strict business transaction." Johnson gave him a playful clap of hand on shoulder. "But I know you've a choice plum in this ship business and naturally I'd like a bite at it. I'm envious, my dear fellow. Now, we'll say no more of that; I don't continue to annoy a man when he's declined to sell. It's near luncheon time; come along to the club with me to-day."

"Thanks, but I can't accept. I have matters to look after immediately."

"Well, some other time then. And remember, you give our bank first consideration of any loans. Mr. Andrews, our assistant-cashier, informed me that you have agreed to open an account with us, which we appreciate. If your loan will be of any size, all I ask is that you give us a day or so of notice.

"It will be a hundred and fifty or two hundred thousand," Stokes stated.

"About when would you want it, do you think?"

"Along in February sometime, probably."

"All right, Stokes. If you should want it before, let me know; I think we'll have no trouble in arranging it, and there will be no need running out west to get it, you understand."

When the ship-builder had gone, Johnson sat down to breathe freely. He wiped the perspiration from his brow. He recognized that he had nearly stepped into a nice mess in trying to put the screws on Stokes, who proved that he was a man one could not take liberties with; but by hastily swinging around the banker had smoothed out his case. Stokes had a fighting eye: he would have done exactly what he said about replacing local labor, operating a boarding-house and so on. He had not been bluffed for a single second. Johnson heaved a sigh of relief at the thought of having escaped the storm he would have brought down upon himself from the working-men, cheap hotel-keepers, merchants and the rest.

"This fellow Stokes is altogether too independent," he presently remarked aloud, however, with a growing indignation at what the man had threatened in reprisal. "It's time he was taken down a peg. If we get this loan, we'll see if we can't put him in his place."

He began to speculate on the possibilities of such a circumstance. At the end of ten minutes he rang up Farrington on the telephone and invited him to luncheon. Farrington accepted—he always accepted when others paid the bill. During the meal later on Johnson informed him that he had interviewed Stokes and that the latter refused to sell a single share of stock.

"The hog! Wants to keep it all for himself!" Farrington replied, unfolding his napkin and setting his lips in a thin line.

"But listen! There's a new angle to the affair. Stokes Brothers will be wanting to borrow some money in a couple of months or so and there may be our chance. I'll inform Main and Derland that there's nothing doing in the stock; that lets them out. You and I will then handle the loan personally—don't want it in our banks for sufficiently good reasons—and see if we can't fix things so that afterwards we may develop the lead."

"Good, very good, very good, indeed!" little Mr. Farrington, of the Lumber and Cotton Bank, replied with a smile appearing upon his shriveled visage. "That will be even better than a purchase of stock, and once the loan is made and properly secured there should be a way of bringing Stokes Brothers to the mark."

"Don't fool yourself that Stokes is a simpleton; he's not," Johnson warned.

Farrington sniffed.

"What difference does it make what he is if he's tied hand and foot. We'll demand for collateral his stock, or a majority of it. Then it will be our business to force sale of it. If we can't devise an issue on which to enjoin the business, attach company accounts in our banks, or otherwise lock up its proceeds about the time the note comes due, you and I had better retire. Huh, with Stokes Brothers' funds handled in our banks, we'll know to a dollar where the concern stands. If it has the cash ready, the latter must be tied up legally for twenty-four hours to allow action on the paper. After that we'll have the stock, take over charge of the business, and Stokes Brothers can sue its head off in the courts about it if it wants to."

"Supposing this Stokes insists on giving a mortgage?"

"Well, we'll insist on a stock collateral," Farrington grinned. "Mark my words, he won't want the bother of a plaster on the property."

With a nod Johnson helped himself to some cold chicken.

"And all can be done legally."

"All legally, all legally. And I imagine our Stokes

friends will learn some of the possibilities of the law of which heretofore they were ignorant." Farrington pinched his nose in thought over the idea. "I presume they have no more notion than the average business man of what can be done by legal procedure. Johnson, this looks better and better."

He laid down his fork to rub his hands and beam at his fellow banker.

"The man hadn't left my office over a minute before I perceived an opportunity in a loan," the latter stated. "And he was so arrogant in the matter of letting any of us into the business that I have no scruples in making what profit we can out of the situation. Really, these outsiders must be taught a lesson."

He regarded Farrington with a grave air. Farrington nodded with equal gravity. It was not well for people like Stokes Brothers to flout the powers that be.

"We'll teach 'em," the little man said, with a tightening of lips. "We should have had that ship business, anyway."

"Look out, there's Main!" Johnson presently exclaimed. "Just coming in. No mention of this before him, of course. Let him and Derland find their own apples—and Broussard declared himself altogether out of the deal the other day."

"That rake!" Farrington snarled. "I'd like to get him where I could break him!"

The other sighed sympathetically.

"So would I—but it's out of the question.

Treachery personified! I'd rejoice if he left Martinsport for good. In a way, one feels contaminated in associating with a man of such natural depravity."

"Called me an old scamp!"

"Deplorable. Yet what can be done." Johnson frowned in annoyance. "He's incorrigible—and worse, secretive. I just heard he cleaned up a quarter of a million on Bethlehem, heard it from a reliable source, and there's never been a peep from him that he had any of the stock. Picked it up at around one-fifty. Never gave a hint at the time that he thought it would be a good thing."

A look of pain crept into the lineaments of Mr. Farrington's face. He closed his eyes as if suffering.

"A quarter of a million! Did that scoundrel make that much on Bethlehem Steel?" he groaned, combing his white chin whisker. "It does appear at times as if the wicked prospered."

"Well, we could do very well without him in Martinsport. Unprincipled—but here's Main!"

The head of the gas company had made his way through the dining-room, speaking now and again to the occupants of some table, until his eyes fell on the pair of bankers. He stopped beside their table.

"Sit down and join us," Johnson invited.

"I'm eating with those men over yonder," Main answered. "Well, what did you learn from Stokes? You were to have seen him this morning, I think."

His heavy jowls spread over the edge of his collar, pressing it down, as he looked at them. Towering above the diminutive Farrington, his bulk seemed huge. The little financier silently devoted himself to his luncheon.

"Saw him and there's no stock for sale," Johnson responded. "Broussard was right on that. And Stokes was as lofty about it as you please."

"Humph. Is that all?"

"I'm afraid so, Main. He wouldn't hear of the idea of letting us in." Johnson shook his head, then took a sip of his iced-tea.

For a little the standing man considered them, as a bull might regard a pair of dogs he mistrusted.

"What are you fellows concocting then?" he demanded. "You had your heads together as I came along. I suppose you're keeping something back about the matter that Derland and I are entitled to know. Remember that it was agreed we were all to be in on this Stokes killing, if there be any. No flimflam goes. We'll take a hand mighty quick if we find you're holding out on us."

Johnson lifted a guileless round face.

"Suppose you see Stokes yourself, if you think I persuaded him to part with any of his stock," he said. Then he added emphatically, "You'll discover that Stokes Brothers is doing all the holding out that's being done—and you're welcome to any stock you can pry loose."

"Humph," Main grunted again.

"By the way, cotton's off ten points to-day," Johnson stated, idly.

"Sold yesterday what I was carrying. Thought a slump about due. Where are you, Farrington?"

"I unloaded a week ago."

"Missed a little then, but not much."

Main moved on towards the table where he was to eat.

III

A FALLING PLANK

ONE morning early in April, of the following spring, Frederic Stokes and the gentleman who had previously owned the site, Mr. Willard, conversed at a spot in the shipyard near the water. They had been moving about the plant, observing the work going on and had now halted at this place. It was open and therefore insured privacy.

The harbor lay before them. Several steamships rested at anchor in the water between the two piers, taking on coal from barges moored alongside. Launches sped to and fro about the basin on business of their own, their exhausts pop-popping industriously. A tug was towing a Scandinavian four-master away from a pier out towards the channel.

Near the men loomed the stern of a building ship, half-concealed by scaffolding, a-ring with the blows of hammers. Farther on the ribbed skeleton of a second vessel under construction stretched its huge hollow frame parallel to the first. A pungent smell of new pine scented the air. The multitudinous sounds of industry arose everywhere about the shipyard.

"You appear to be driving the work," Mr. Willard stated. "This boat ought to be ready to launch soon." And he indicated with his cane the nearer vessel.

"In six weeks—if we're not blocked by trouble," Stokes replied, grimly.

"Labor trouble?"

"Yes, labor and other kinds. Mostly other kinds, so far, have been happening, but there are signs that we'll get a dose of labor worry presently. Somebody's stirring things up in order to put Stokes Brothers in a hole."

"I heard indirectly something to that effect," Willard remarked, "so I came over to apprise you of the fact. There's a move on foot to hamstring your business."

Stokes swung about so as to face the speaker.

"When did you learn that?" he asked, quickly.

"Yesterday. Nothing definite, but the word was dropped in my hearing. I intend to look into the matter a little farther. Having interested myself in bringing you here, I was therefore interested in knowing that some one is after your company with a knife; the news displeased me."

Mr. Willard announced the fact in a tone of voice that carried a slight trace of annoyance. As already said, he was an elderly gentleman. His spare figure, however, was straight, his cheeks retained a clear fresh color. With upper lip shaven in the fashion of an earlier generation he wore a short, white beard that gave his countenance a benign and

almost ministerial aspect. But a keen glint was in
his eyes and the impression of mildness was somewhat lessened when he thrust a long, slim, black,
piratical-looking cigar into a corner of his mouth.
He shut his lips tightly, which cocked the cigar up
at a rakish angle.

"I never did admire this Martinsport bunch of
money-bushwhackers," said he. "Nothing would
rejoice me so much as to see you get out your bat-
tle-ax and slice off some of the fat from whoever's
trying to do you up—I suppose it's one or all of
them.

"Your statement that you had heard a rumor I
was being attacked makes my suspicion a certainty,"
Stokes said. "For some time I've suspected there
was a design to injure our business. Things went
along all right until about the first of March, then
troubles began that could be explained only on that
assumption. We were then ahead of our scheduled
rate of construction; we've since lost that gain and
gone behind. And, mark you, this happened in
spite of the fact that we are employing more men
now than earlier!"

"What were the specific causes of loss?" Willard
asked.

"Men shirking, delays, accidents. The superintendent first called my attention to matters a month
ago, wanting to know if any one was deliberately
working to prevent building of the ships. He had
an idea there might be German agents at work to
stop construction or destroy the plant. He's con-

vinced that at least some of the accidents have been mischievous, and is sure there's been meddling with the men. Not all of them, but with a number, enough to slow up things. He quietly learns who are the slackers and we replace them with new workmen as rapidly as possible. A section of scaffolding fell one night; the watchman swore he saw nothing or heard nothing until the accident happened. I have a half a dozen guards patrolling the yard of nights now. Another instance: we had to rip out a deck section—bad material and bad construction both. Mulhouse discovered it before it was all down; and we fired the foreman in charge. No stupidity in the case, couldn't have been. Another time a lot of lumber was sawn wrong lengths; too short. And so on. Everything but fire. Somebody put a row of augur-holes in the stern-post of that boat just starting over there—ruined it, of course. Will have to jerk it down and set up another, and the timber, like that of the ribs, is all specially sawn to shape. It will take a week or ten days to replace it. That happened only last night. I'm going to extend the fence along the water, for whoever did the job got into the yard from the water side. I thought at first what occurred might be due to spite of some disgruntled workmen, but I changed my mind presently. The delay and damage was too well-devised and too continuous. As Mulhouse maintains, it has a look of German agents' work.

"They would either burn or blow up your ships

at once," Mr. Willard answered, reflectively. "Were the workmen you've discharged of German nationality?"

"No, on the contrary the naturalized Germans employed are steady and reliable. The men responsible for delays or mistakes, whenever found, were American or French or Italian by birth. A number of them were from New Orleans; a few live here in Martinsport. The great bulk of the carpenters, understand, are straight, but a few malicious men can make plenty of trouble for all and cut down immensely the effectiveness of all."

"I think, Stokes, the nationality of the men discharged does away with any theory of German agents, unless the latter are working very cunningly. The rumor I heard confirms the idea that the little war you have on hand is being conducted by some one purely for profit."

"You spoke of Martinsport bushwhackers," Stokes exclaimed, with a sudden inspiration. "Now that I think of it, it doesn't seem unlikely. Several men wanted to buy stock, and gave me a threat or two when I refused. I felt their hostility to our enterprise at the time, but supposed it was only a passing exasperation of the moment. They've since shown no feeling, and indeed accommodated us by a loan."

"Who did?" Willard demanded, abruptly.

"Johnson and Farrington."

"Their banks, or the men personally?"

"The two men. They stated that the directors of

their institutions were opposed to making the loan while our company was but yet newly established— at least for two hundred thousand, which was the amount I wanted. But the men stood ready to furnish it personally."

"Rot! Their banks could have handled a hundred thousand apiece without difficulty."

"I suspected so, but I didn't care," Stokes stated.

"They have something up their sleeves. How did they try to tie you up?"

Stokes laughed.

"I see you know them! First, they wanted both a mortgage on the property and our stock as collateral. I requested them to get their feet down on the ground and said I'd give a mortgage. That brought out their real demand—the stock. The loan was finally arranged by my putting up half our capitalization, stock for two hundred and fifty thousand."

"That was what they wanted. They'll see if they can't hold that collateral by forfeiture."

"That's what I wanted, too—and let them try to monkey with us if they've a feeling that way. We'll build a fire under them if they do. I wouldn't have put a mortgage on the plant in a thousand years for those fellows."

"They're slippery," the visitor remarked.

"All right. They seemed fair enough about it, but I was taking no chances. If it's their scheme to get a strangle-hold on the business, let them proceed; but I'm here to say that Stokes Brothers has no intention of being strangled, scuttled, or anything else. But certainly these two gentlemen wouldn't instigate the criminal interference with our work that's occurring, in the hope of preventing us from meeting our note when due."

Willard shook his head. He removed his cigar, inspected it and again put it in his mouth.

"Oh, no. Johnson and Farrington don't operate in that way," he stated, with finality. "You can lay aside any suspicion of them being the responsible parties; their activities when they move will take quite another direction, I conjecture."

"Then that leaves me in the dark."

"When did these concealed attacks begin, Stokes?"

"We began to notice the frequency of accidents and delays about the first week in March, with a consequent falling off in the rate of construction."

"And when did you secure this loan?"

"Well, towards the latter end of February," Stokes made answer. "Since you bring the two facts together, it appears a striking coincidence that our troubles began to multiply almost immediately after the loan was made."

"Very singular, indeed. But though the circumstance points at the two bankers, you need have no fear they would mix up in anything of the kind. Nevertheless there may be a connection between the happenings."

"You seem to have something definite in mind."

"Well, I haven't," Willard said. "I'm merely

indulging my habit of seeking causes in effects. If there's any relation between your borrowing money late in February and the beginning of secret assaults on your property a week or so afterwards, it narrows the inquiry. It brings the matter down to a point where you can ask yourself who besides the parties concerned know of the loan, how they are interested in it, why should it inspire a desire on the part of others to damage you, what do they hope to gain by it. I think I can answer the last question at once. Somebody else is after your business—always, of course, counting on the theory there is a relation between the facts."

"I perceive this is a complex little fight, figuring that Johnson and Farrington are after my scalp, too."

"The latter is a contingency it will be well to make allowance for," Willard replied.

Stokes pulled his hat lower over his eyes and gazed grimly at the ships and about the yard. The sounds of labor, the moving figures of men, the general air of industry, appeared to give him a new sense of assurance.

"I didn't come down here into this country and start this plant for local vultures to fight over," said he. "If war is what they want, war is what they shall get. Let us go back to the office. To begin with, I'll have the yard strung with electric lights and the guards armed with shot-guns. Perhaps a load of buckshot will discourage the night-prowlers. I'll have Mocket, the book-keeper, secure a permit this afternoon for firearms in the yard."

"Place a detective or two among the workmen to learn who is supplying the money," Willard suggested.

"Yes, I'll do that. I'll send to an agency for men to-day or to-morrow. They should be able to get wind of things."

At the office door Willard, after a few more words, stepped into the motor car that awaited him there.

"Make the pirates, whoever they are, pay for their fun," said he. "I'm running up to Chicago and Detroit for a few days, but when I return I'll look into this affair a bit myself."

And he was driven away.

About two o'clock that afternoon a plank fell from a low scaffolding being erected about the frame of the second ship. Stokes chanced to be passing underneath at the instant and it struck him to earth. Workmen carried him to the office, where a doctor and ambulance were hastily summoned. Though the fall of the plank had not been great, it was sufficient to break his collar-bone and left arm, besides dealing him a severe glancing blow upon the head. He had regained consciousness before the arrival of the physician and despite his pain had given his stenographer instructions of a private nature regarding the business. Then he was rushed to his home.

IV

WHO IS THE ENEMY?

If it were possible to observe the course of a telegraphed communication as a visible phenomenon, a message that began at Martinsport might have been seen as a succession of flashes between points sparking its way from city to city, in long leaps, up and up northwest across the continent until it ended in a final flash in Seattle. There a man in an office read the message and took down a telephone receiver. Back in the timber of the Cascade Range, in a small heavily wooded little valley, another man answered the ring. He in turn went to the door and called across to the cook-shack. The cook replied, then yelled to a youngster outside, put a doughnut in the latter's hand when he ran up, spoke a word of instruction and shooed the little boy out of the shack by a flap of his apron.

"Now skip—make your feet fly!" he commanded. "Tell Bob Stokes that Mac says he's wanted at the telephone in a hurry. You'll find him down where they're loading cars. Don't fool by the way, or I'll warm your pants with a butter-paddle. Run!"

The lad trotted off, stuffing his mouth as he

43

went. Five minutes later a tall, tanned, blue-eyed young fellow strode up the slope and entered the office. The still more youthful book-keeper nodded his head towards the telephone.

"Hurry-up call from J. C., Bob," he stated.

"All right. Probably about that extra-length stuff he wants."

He crossed to the telephone, gave the handle a spin and called for the Seattle office connection. Then he lighted a cigarette while waiting, stuck a toe into the stomach of a cat lying just by his feet and wiggled it there, then rolled his eyes about upon the boyish book-keeper.

"When was the divorce, Mac?" he inquired.

"What divorce?" The book-keeper regarded him suspiciously.

"I perceive that the missives you're getting this week are encased in baby pink envelopes, while those you've been having were in blue. And the handwriting on them also appears strange and weird. Hence, a new dame."

A bright color appeared in the other's cheeks.

"By golly, a fellow can't have even a new girl without the whole camp knowing it!" he exclaimed.

"Pretty?"

"Some apple, Bob, believe me! Met her last time I was down, and after the first look I fell for her like a thousand of brick."

"But where, oh, where was Annie?"

"Annie, your boot!" was the disgusted reply.

"The other one's name wasn't Annie, but Seraphina. She ditched me for——"

"Hold! Stokes ordered. "Say that name again and say it slowly. Seraph—I'll bet, with a handle like that, she was as short and dumpy as one of Bill's puddings."

The book-keeper sniffed disdainfully.

"You lose. She was thin and—and—mercenary! I started to tell you she ditched me for a fellow with a yellow auto. Ditched me cold, after all the money I'd spent, too."

Stokes shook his head sadly, the telephone receiver still held to his ear.

"Heartless, fickle woman!" quoth he. "But I suppose the new one is as sincere as she's beautiful, especially when the girlie is gazing soulfully over her nut sundae into Mac's burning orbs, as he relates his hairbreadth adventures up here in the woods."

"Go to the devil!" the boy ejaculated, with a red face.

With eyes fixed upon the ceiling Stokes continued in a declamatory voice:

"Ah, those tender looks! Ah, those blissful drugstore romances, half heartache, half soda-water fizz! I've been there, my son; I've known the same sweet sorrow. I've shivered with that same mixture of joy and ice-cream. . . . Hello, that you, John? . . . What's that; hurt! . . . Yes, I can go at once. As soon as I shake myself out of these clothes and boots I'll hop into my car and start down. I'll

be in town in three hours if I come in on one
wheel. . . . Tough luck for Fred. Hope to heaven
it's no more than busted bones, though that's bad
enough. Might have killed the old boy! . . . All
right; see to my ticket and Pullman. I'll be there
by six, or know why."

He clapped the receiver in place and turned to
the book-keeper, who had listened with growing
concern on his face.

"What happened to F. W.?" the latter asked,
quickly.

"Broken shoulder—accident. I'm starting for
Martinsport immediately. Rustle out and bring
Barney, so I can give him a last word. Then bring
my car to the door, please. I'll have to change my
clothes and run through the papers in my desk.
Must be away from here in fifteen minutes."

At the end of that period both Barney, the woods
boss, and the runabout awaited him. To the former he gave a number of instructions.

"J. C. will be running up here often," he said,
"and he'll keep in touch with you constantly by
'phone. Mac, explain my absence to Aitken. Tell
him to keep sawing the stuff he's on; I haven't
a moment more to spare, or I'd see him myself.
Keep J. C. advised of everything—he'll doubtless
be along immediately. Look over the commissary
lists with Jorgensen that I was going to check up.
And find out why that new saw isn't here, and give
the railroad a poke. Barney, keep the men driving
on the trees—better shift the log track where we

talked of. If Pete's leg doesn't appear to get healed
as it should, send him down to a hospital and tell
him not to worry about the cost. Well, I'm starting. It's up to you boys to make the lumber spout.
Luck with you!" and off he drove, waving a hand
behind.

As good as his word, he reached Seattle by six,
finding his brother awaiting him in the company
office. John Stokes, the elder of the three brothers,
and known as J. C., was about thirty-eight—ten
years older than Bob. Both he and Frederic Stokes
sometimes jokingly called the young fellow a "family after-thought," but were exceedingly proud of
the strong, active, hustling junior. Stokes Brothers was considered a coming firm, with shrewdness
and nerve and "pep."

"You can leave to-night and be in Martinsport in
four days if you make train connections," J. C. said,
after Bob had read the telegram announcing the
accident to their brother. "I had Voss look up
the timetables and schedule the best route. If there
had been any way to arrange the matter I would
have gone myself, but I'm up to my neck in deals
here. Anyway, a few days would have done no
good. Fred may be laid up two or three months."

"Yes, I'm the one to go," Bob answered. 'What's
this about something in his last letters that you
spoke of over the 'phone?"

The older man adjusted his nose-glasses and drew
forward a file of correspondence.

"These letters came this week," said he, "the

last one only this morning, so you haven't seen them. Fred writes of the trouble with men he's been having, and of the numerous accidents in the yard. States they're apparently malicious; his superintendent thinks so, at any rate. Is convinced some one's deliberately injuring the company, but isn't sure whether it's German agents or aggrieved workmen or who. Take the correspondence along with you and read it on the train. You can mail it back from some point along the road."

"Very well. Somebody dropped the board on Fred intentionally then; the wire says a falling plank hit him."

"Wouldn't be surprised, if his suspicions in the matter are right. But no disgruntled workman would be responsible in the sense the word implies. As Fred lists the occurrences in his letters, it looks like a systematic campaign of attack by the I. W. W.'s. But by what he's learned none of the workmen are in that outfit. So somebody else is behind it."

"Perhaps German agents, as the superintendent suggests," Bob said, at once.

"Well, that's what you'll have to find out. Fred will be able to tell you something more if he's able to talk when you arrive. If not, you'll have to dig it out. There may be another explanation: Fred wrote when he first went to Martinsport that there was apparent hostility to us by some local people because we had picked up the only shipyard site. Not likely they would start anything as raw as trying to sandbag our business, but bear the fact in mind. You'll have to consider every possibility and run down every clew. And if any one is really making a dirty, underhanded fight, look out for yourself—he'll try to get you as he got Fred."

"Let him—or they, or it, whichever it is," Bob snapped out. "Let 'em try it; I can use the rough stuff, too. But what the deuce would any persons besides enemy agents want to put us down and out for?"

The older brother tapped the desk with forefinger.

"To get our business—bankrupt us, break us, lay us flat and then secure the assets of the concern far below what they are worth. Martinsport no doubt realizes by now that we've a little mint there. Any man who stops to figure will see that the profits of the first two boats will pay back every dollar of capital invested, and that afterwards everything will be velvet."

"Well, I've been up in the timber and haven't given the ship end of it much thought," Bob remarked. "Where's the pinch? How can any one nip us?"

"We borrowed two hundred thousand down there."

"Yes, I know. Go ahead."

"Our credit here was about all used in swinging the purchase of that big Oregon tract of timber we bought. When Fred learned definitely he could get the money he needed at Martinsport, why, we went ahead and bought the tract. That left us just enough cash to keep the business going in good shape until we could begin to cut some of the new stuff and realize."

"I remember."

"But with everything tied up, we'll be able to pay the Martinsport loan only when the first ship is sold. The loan will fall due about a month after Fred's scheduled date for completion of the vessel."

"The light begins to glimmer in my brain," said Bob.

"His recent letters report that because of the delays, accidents and so on, which he believed engineered, the work was dropping behind schedule. And now he's clear out of the game, probably strapped up in a plaster cast. Things will be kept moving of course by those in charge, but not as if Fred were on hand. If a ship is not finished and sold, we'll have a note of two hundred thousand to meet and no money, unless we let go the timber again."

"We need that timber; we'll not let go of that," said Bob.

"No. And we can't raise anything on it at present. It's carrying a good load as it is. Once our mill is into the stuff, the money will come in fast enough at prices lumber is bringing and will continue to bring. That was a good buy; we must hang on to it. So it's up to you to see that first ship is launched."

"As I remember, the loan was made on stock collateral, not by mortgage," Bob reflected.

"Yes—I've not forgotten that. Fred didn't want, a mortgage. Of course, we can do so if it comes to a last shot, though if it becomes known some one's injuring our property the matter will be more difficult. And there's a chance, too, of selling a ship on a substantial payment down before it's finished, since competition for ships is brisk. I didn't say any one could break us; I'm explaining the state of affairs in case some person has such an object in view. But we might have to do a bit of lively financing at the last minute if we make no provision."

Bob smiled, then finally laughed.

"You always do make provision, though," said he. "The way you're reciting the 'pros' and 'cons' shows me you've been employing a few minutes of spare time in cogitations."

For a moment John Stokes also smiled.

"Since receiving Fred's letters, yes," said he, "and since getting the telegram this afternoon I've given my mind to the subject. Fred, I imagine, has had something ready in case the holders of our notes tried to take any undue advantage of the situation; he hinted as much when the loan was made. You'll find out and let me know what it is. I think I can guarantee that Stokes Brothers will continue to do business right along."

Bob suddenly jumped up and began to stride to and fro across the room.

"Do you think the men who loaned this money are making us the trouble? Could they be such damned ruffians as to have Fred laid out cold by a plank to gain their ends?" he demanded.

"You're going there to learn that, as I've already stated."

"I'll find out, never worry. Somebody shall pay for nearly killing him—it might have killed him! I'll discover who it was if I have to use a fine-comb on the whole town. No one can put across a dirty, murderous trick like that on Fred and not pay for it."

"Right, Bob. We'll sharpen our knives, and if the thing was really deliberate the man shall pay dearly for it," John Stokes affirmed, with a sudden compression of his lips. "There's only one treatment for bushwhackers!"

All at once Bob stopped in his stride.

"The men who loaned the money are bankers, I recall," he said. "Isn't that right?"

"Yes."

"Then surely they wouldn't be such scoundrels!"

"One finds it difficult to believe so—we'll give them the benefit of the doubt until you discover the culprits. But, in any case, we'll be prepared so that they can't take advantage of us, even if they're not mixed up in it. They might feel so disposed."

"Possibly it's German agents, after all."

"No telling. But trust no one but Fred—and Willard. Do you remember him? No, I don't believe you ever made his acquaintance. He gave us the tip on the ship business there and sold us the site. Used to know father, and has dropped in here at the office occasionally when he's in the west. Interested with the West Coast Mill and Development people."

"Big man, then."

"Yes. Has several lumber concerns in the south and other interests over the country. He lives in Detroit, but spends a good deal of time in Martinsport because of the climate. Outside of him, there's no one you can trust. Now, I think that's about all. We'll go up to dinner, for Martha and the kiddies are expecting you, of course, to say good-by. Martha has a lot of messages for you to carry to Alice, who'll be worried to death by Fred's injuries. We can talk a bit more after eating, then you'll have time to pack your trunk and the like. Train leaves at ten-fifteen."

He arose and pulled shut the roller top of his desk.

"Where's Jim Flanagan—Snohomish Jim?" Bob asked, all at once.

"Cruising out Number Three tract."

"When will he finish?"

"In two or three days. He's nearly through, I judge."

"Can you spare him, John?" Bob inquired, meditatively.

"I guess so. Was going to send him down to run through the Oregon timber again. What about him?"

Pausing to light his pipe, Bob gathered up the correspondence which he was to read on the train and stuffed it in his pocket.

"Send him along down after me when he comes in," he said. "I'll put him on as a carpenter and if he doesn't nose out something, I miss my guess. Tell him he's to find the fellow who got Fred—that's all that will be necessary. He's particularly fond of Fred. He can hammer nails, I suppose."

"Enough to pass as a carpenter, I think."

Bob nodded.

"Jim's the man I want. Have him shuck off his woods togs and make up as a workman and tell him to lay in a supply of palm-leaf fans, too, as he's going where it's warm. Ticket him through and he'll show up all right even if he does cross a few 'wet' states; he always arrives on time, drunk or sober."

"I'll see him properly started," John smiled.

The two brothers departed. It was nearly seven o'clock as they left the office and the homeward flow of folk had subsided, leaving the streets comparatively empty. At the telegraph stand near the elevators at the entrance of the building they turned aside to dispatch a message to the Martinsport office notifying it of Bob's leaving and another to Fred's wife.

"Two wires for you just came in," the operator informed John Stokes. And he passed them across the counter.

"From Alice. Says, 'Fred resting easy,'" John stated, handing the first to his brother.

"Good boy! I'll bet he'll disgust the doctor by getting well and whole again in double-quick time."

His satisfaction was quick to appear. He clicked his tongue between his teeth, clapped his brother John on the shoulder and added a word about no one being able to kill a Stokes with a mere piece of lumber, the Stokes family having invented lumber.

"This one is from the office," John said, who had been scanning the second telegram. "Here it is: 'Imperative another member firm come Martinsport immediately have just learned injunction pending to tie up plant will engage lawyer to try prevent it and will keep work going till arrival await answer— E. Durand.' Time you were getting down there, Bob," John continued, with his jaw growing hard. "Not satisfied with laying Fred out with a lot of broken bones, whoever's managing this conspiracy is going to jump us and garrote us legally too if they can, along with their other dirty work. At any rate, a suit will give you a chance to find out who is concerned, if you probe deep enough. Damn 'em, once we get our claws on their windpipe there'll be no mercy!"

"Exactly so, none, none whatever. We go the full limit now," Bob answered, "both ways and across."

"And don't hesitate to draw for any money you'll want. Wire me, that's all. I'll see that you have it. And keep me advised every day; do the wiring yourself in our private code. I'm not going to sit idle."

Bob read the second telegram again.

"Who's this Durand?" he inquired.

"Office man, I guess. Appears efficient and not afraid of responsibility, by his messages. He sent the first, of the accident."

"I'll buy him a cigar and raise his salary for this," said Bob. "He deserves it for standing up to the fight."

V

THE GIRL IN CHARGE

THE wall clock in the outer office of Stokes Brothers had just struck four when Robert Stokes opened the screen door and entered. The offices were in the end nearest the shipyard gate of a long, low building covered with galvanized iron, the greater part of which was used as a warehouse. On his arrival in Martinsport Stokes had gone immediately to his brother's dwelling, where to his immense relief he found his brother Frederic suffering no injuries beyond those of broken bones and elated that the young fellow had come. An hour's discussion of business before luncheon and another parley afterwards of equal length—the limit set by the doctor—resulted in Bob's going to town and dispatching a long telegram to John Stokes at Seattle. Bob had then pursued his way to the shipyard.

As he advanced to the counter that fenced off half of the office, he directed an appraising glance about. It had the usual furnishings of such a place. A few chairs sat outside the counter; inside were filing-cases, safe, tables and the like. On a high stool a thin, middle-aged man worked on a ledger lying open on the tall desk before him. He did

57

not look up at Stokes' entrance but continued to ply his pen steadily and smoothly, showing only his profile. Standing by the safe and gazing morosely out a window was a second person, a short bullet-headed youth.

He presently turned his head about to view the visitor, without troubling to remove his hands from his trousers' pockets or to alter his position. Neither his features nor his apparel impressed Stokes favorably. His forehead was low, his ears prominent, and a half-smoked cigarette hung from his lower lip. A scowl, apparently at the interruption to his thoughts, darkened his face as he eyed the stranger. He wore a pink shirt, with the sleeves rolled to his elbows, a flaring yellow-and-green striped scarf, and trousers of bright blue serge—a color scheme of contrasting violence beside the plain black of the book-keeper, or Stokes' own simple gray.

Stokes pushed back his straw hat and scrutinized the other. A suspicion had instantly begun to eddy in his mind. If the firm's enemies had a tool inside the shipyard, this fellow was in all probability the man. He had all the ear-marks of one who would sell out his employers for money. He was in the office where he knew what was being done and could thus pass on the information to others. Without himself directly acting, he could advise the plotters so that they might cunningly prepare and carry out their veiled attacks. Bob felt a quick beat of satisfaction; he had opened up a lead the minute he had set foot in the shipyard.

The other spoke.

"Nothing doing. Not buying anything to-day."

The utterance was manifestly intended to forestall and dispose of any salesmanship line of talk,
He had evidently decided Stokes had something to
sell. And, moreover, in his present sour spirits he
viewed the other's cheerful mien with strong dis-
favor.

"Are you the manager here?" Stokes inquired.

"No."

"What is your official position, then?"

"I'm a clerk—and nothing official about it,
either."

At this minute the book-keeper laid down his pen
and swung about on his stool. He wore nose-
glasses, through which he peered at Stokes with the
vague fixedness of the near-sighted person. These,
and his thin serious face, gave him an aspect of
professorial gravity, in marked contrast to the
youth's air of pugnacious gloom. But he displayed
no indication of interjecting himself into the discussion.

Bob Stokes placed his hat upon the counter, drew
forth a handkerchief and wiped the perspiration
from his face.

"So you're not buying anything to-day?" he remarked.

"No."

"Well, what are you doing for Stokes Brothers
besides dragging at that cigarette on your lip?"
Bob inquired.

The other thrust out his jaw and drew down his bullet head, as if he were about to butt.

"Say, are you trying to start something around here?" he demanded, in a hostile tone.

"I'll decide that presently." Stokes tossed one of his business cards upon the counter. "After you've taken a look at that. And if I start something, I'll finish it. Now step up here and glue your glim on this pasteboard and learn that courtesy is as necessary in an office as ink—even to a man with something to sell. Stokes Brothers, for that matter, sell things too."

"Humph," the clerk grunted.

After a first surprised stare on hearing Bob's speech he advanced doggedly, picked up the card, and read the engraved name. For a little his expression retained its obstinacy, as if he did not catch the card's full significance, then his neck and face and ears went bright crimson.

He laid the card down.

"You're right," said he. "And I've tied a can on myself."

He began to roll down his sleeves, with a sort of determination. As he crossed to a hook and removed his coat and hat, Stokes watched him interestedly.

"Where are you going?" he asked.

"To look for a new job. I'm fired, ain't I?"

"Not by me."

The clerk gazed at him in bewilderment.

"You mean you're keeping me after that talk I handed you, Mr. Stokes?"

"We can use you yet, I guess."

The other continued to stare, while the fact percolated through his brain. In one hand he held his hat, in the other his coat trailed on the floor. He looked as it he had received a jolt between the eyes.

"Huh, I thought I'd queered myself for good," said he.

"Well, you haven't—yet."

The slight intonation of the last word went unheeded by the clerk. Under ordinary circumstances Stokes might have let him proceed on his way unstopped, but convinced as he was that the young fellow was worth watching he resolved to retain him for purposes of observation.

"Much obliged to you, Mr. Stokes; I'll remember what you said about courtesy," the youth stated, somewhat sheepishly.

"All right, Andrews—your name is Andrews, I think?"

"Yes, sir. Bill Andrews."

"And yours, Mocket?" Stokes added, turning to the book-keeper.

The latter lowered himself from his stool, removed his nose-glasses and walked forward.

"Pleased to make your acquaintance, Mr. Stokes," he said, extending a hand. "We were not aware you had arrived. It was a very unfortunate accident that occurred to your brother; he's resting comfortably, I understand."

With his glasses off he looked a trifle younger. The seriousness of his lean, smooth-shaven face was relieved by a black brilliancy of the eyes which was not lessened by their impaired vision. His hair thinned in front in premature baldness, Stokes observed, partly accounted for his ascetic appearance.

For a few minutes Stokes chatted with him of his brother's condition, at the same time noting that Andrews who had hung up his coat and hat again continued to stare his way in contemplative silence, his hands once more in his pockets, his head lowered in bull-dog fashion. Bob renewed his resolution to smoke out that young fellow.

Presently he nodded to Mocket and moved towards the door of the inner office. There was a faint, hurried swish of skirts as he approached it. When he stepped inside, a young lady sat at a typewriter desk in apparent absorption in a letter but with evident signs of just that instant having seated herself. Stokes was confident that she had barely gained the chair before his entrance. For one thing, there was a suspicious pink in her face.

"I heard you, so you needn't pretend to have been reading the letter," he said, grinning. "You had hopped over to the door when Andrews and I were exchanging ideas, ready to burst out and stop the mêlée if there was one. Isn't that the case, Miss Durand? You're Miss Durand, of course, who sent the telegrams."

The color in the girl's cheeks had heightened as she was apprised of the failure of her retreat. In some embarrassment she arose and shook hands with Stokes.

"Well, I was there, yes," she acknowledged. "But I wasn't hiding, as might appear. Mr. Andrews didn't know who you were, while I did—I knew you were coming. So when he started to argue I jumped up to tell him your name. I reached the door and was standing in it as he read your card, but neither of you were looking my way. Then I just remained to hear what you had to say regarding your brother—we've all been anxious about him, you know. Finally I realized what you might think if you saw me there in the door listening, and—and retired."

"I'd have thought it nothing out of the way at all," Bob assured her.

"It wouldn't have appeared polite, at any rate," she said.

One would not have called her in the least pretty —that is, pretty in the sense the word is so frequently used to indicate soft regularity of features, without character. Her black hair was thick and rebellious, especially about her small fine ears; her dark eyes glowed from beneath brows level and heavy; her lips were of a warm red, but with a little, curious, upward twitch at one corner. It was this tiny quirk of the mouth that drew one's attention. It gave the face a subtle animation. One grew expectant at seeing it, felt an aroused interest, and was impelled to lift a look to her eyes to seek a meaning.

Bob Stokes seated himself near by.

"My brother tells me that you've been the real manager here since he was injured," he stated. "And I shall write to J. C. at Seattle that E. Durant, who sent those very business-like wires, is not a young man at all as we had supposed." And he smiled as he recalled his words to his brother John that he would buy a cigar for the sender of the messages and give a "raise" in salary. Well, he would see to the salary increase, at any rate.

"I've not been exactly the boss," said she, "But I've helped a little bit in keeping the wheels moving until you came. The correspondence, however, has been largely routine; here are some letters I'm getting out now." She laid her hand on a pile of sheets resting beside her machine. "We had a good supply of material on hand, fortunately, when Mr. Frederic Stokes was hurt, and in addition Mr. Mulhouse, the superintendent, has told me what was needed and I ordered it. And finally I hired and fired a few men, using the common term."

"Hiring and firing is the test of whether one's the boss," he rejoined, with a flicker of amusement.

"The authority didn't actually rest in me, though," she went on. "You see, it's Mr. Mulhouse's business to employ and to discharge workmen, and I only approved formally what he did when he reported the removals. He knew, of course, I was just rubber-stamping them with an O. K."

The odd twitch at the corner of her mouth deepened as if she were about to laugh, or exclaim, or put a question—Bob Stokes could not tell which. But instead of doing any of the three, she remained gazing at him with a veiled dusky look in her eyes, utterly at variance with the rest of her expression, apparently taking stock of this new member of the company and forming unvoiced, private conclusions regarding him and his ability to step into his brother's shoes.

Bob glanced about the room.

"That's Frederic's desk yonder, I suppose," said he. "I'll use it." He arose, went to the door, closed it. "Now we'll get busy—what about this lawsuit you wired of?" he asked, when he had returned. "Has it been started? My brother appeared not to know about it, for he did not speak of it in our talk; nor did I mention the subject, as it would only cause him useless worry. You learned of it since he was hurt, I judge, or about the time, as your telegram was dispatched the same day. Is that correct?"

"Yes; that noon. I intended to inform Mr. Stokes of what I had accidentally heard, but did not get to do so before his mishap."

"Accidentally heard, you say?"

"Quite by chance," she nodded. "A woman of the name of Gaudreault had been doing some sewing for me. Her little boy brought the things home that noon and began talking, saying that his mother would sew no more for anybody soon when they were rich. I was amused. I asked him if they were going to be very rich and he said 'yes,' that his father had found out he owned the ground the shipyard was on and had hired a lawyer to get it. At that, I set out to learn all about the matter. A lawyer has been coming to their house and telling them of the thing, he said. The boy was not very clear, but I discovered enough to know a suit was contemplated on the ground of the man being the rightful heir, or because of imperfect title, or something of that kind. But no suit has yet been brought against the company—I've telephoned the court house every day and been ready to engage an attorney the instant I knew it had been begun."

"I'll look into the matter. Thank you for guarding our interests so carefully. Now tell me, have any more accidents occurred in the yard since my brother has been absent?"

"Nothing of importance, Mr. Stokes."

The young fellow reflected for a little time.

"You were in my brother's confidence to the degree of knowing his opinion about what's been going on here, Miss Durand, because he dictated to you the private letters he wrote our office at Seattle. What do you think about these happenings?"

Her face grew more serious. She hesitated before speaking.

"As Mr. Frederic Stokes stated the case in the correspondence, his view was very convincing," she said. "I've thought about the matter a great deal since he was hurt—and been uneasy. I'm greatly relieved that you're here. And something did happen too to make me anxious. Not an accident, but something else." A shadow of perplexity appeared upon her face, and she stared past him in a sudden intentness of thought. "Yes, I'm quite sure about it."

"What occurred?" he asked.

"It had to do with the letter files there." She pointed at the cases. "Two nights ago some one went through them. I always straighten them at the end of the day, leaving them in order. When I opened one of the drawers yesterday morning, the envelopes in it did not look exactly as they should. A few of them were sticking up more than I ever have them, very little, but yet more. One notices a change like that, or perhaps feels it. You could tell if some one had moved things in your desk, couldn't you?"

"Yes," Stokes replied.

"Well, that was how I knew. And on running through the envelopes I found a letter or two displaced."

"Anything gone?"

"Not that I could discover."

"Were Frederic's confidential letters there?"

The girl shook her head.

"Mr. Stokes took home that correspondence. He said any one who had a mind to do so could pry open one of these windows. But the windows have not been tampered with, so far as I could find."

"Have you any suspicion who ransacked the files?"

Involuntarily her eyes sought the door to the outer office. Then glancing back and perceiving his look on her, she showed a trace of confusion. Afterwards she busied herself tucking up the hair about her ears.

"No," said she, finally.

"Are those men out there trustworthy?" he inquired. "How about Mocket"—she shook her head—"well, Andrews?"

Her lips were compressed and her hands continued busy with her hair. She was not looking at Stokes.

"No," said she, now with a swift furtive glance at him.

"They have keys to the building, of course."

"But not to this door."

Stokes arose and sauntered to one of the windows. He seemed to hear an expelled breath, as of relief. He could almost feel her eyes, veiled by their long black lashes, gazing inscrutably at his back. Her manner when he spoke of Andrews refuted her words—but why was she shielding the fellow? He stared thoughtfully through the open window at the eastern pier. A gentle wind was blowing towards the shipyard. Suddenly he swung about with a dark face. She drew back, showing a flutter of alarm.

"What's this awful smell I'm getting?" he demanded.

The anxiety died out of her eyes; she broke into a laugh.

"Rotting oyster shell at the canneries. You gave me a scare—I thought you had seen something terrible."

Bob Stokes turned again to the window and sniffed.

"I don't need to see it, I smell it," said he.

VI

BOB STOKES INVESTIGATES

BEFORE work stopped that afternoon Bob Stokes made a tour of the yard. He knew nothing about building ships. He knew that he knew nothing about ship-building. However, Mulhouse, the superintendent, an oldish New Englander, possessed in a high degree the knowledge of constructing wooden vessels, that almost forgotten but suddenly revived craft; which was all the business needed. The task confronting the young fellow was of a different character. He must fend off future attacks upon the plant and if possible run the plotters out into the broad light of day.

He located Mulhouse overseeing work on the newer of the boats. After making himself known and chatting for a time on cursory subjects, Bob drew the superintendent aside.

"My brother tells me you believe as he does," said he, "that the delays and the accidents, including his own, which have occurred here are the result of deliberate plotting."

Mulhouse pulled his gray beard and nodded.

"No question of some one causing the trouble," he stated.

"Nothing has happened since he was hurt, though."

"No, but I'm expecting a jab most any time. They may try to get you or me next."

"You're no wiser yet as to who dropped the plank on my brother, I take it?"

"No. Haven't an inkling. There's always more or less loose lumber lying about on the scaffolds. A fellow could give a board a shove off with his foot as F. W. went along underneath and be at work again in an instant. The other men, being busy, wouldn't see."

"There can be no large number of men disloyal to our interests, or you would know it, wouldn't you?"

"Yes. It would become known. We've discharged several workmen, those responsible for delays," Mulhouse said. "I doubt if there are more than two or three in the pay of the outsiders, and they have a leader, of course. I still have a feeling, Mr. Stokes, that there's some German alien's hand in this, though your brother's opinion is different. I'm watching a man or two."

Bob Stokes observed for a little time the carpenters at work on the skeleton hull. An incessant hammering went on along the length of the building vessel; the intermittent screech of a planer sounded from somewhere in the yard; there came an occasional dull clap of dropped boards.

"F. W. has an idea he wants us to try out," Bob remarked, presently. "He's been thinking conditions over since he's been laid up and believes the way to prevent future trouble is to enlist the workmen on our side."

Mulhouse drew out a pocket-knife. He bent and picked up a stick, then began to whittle.

"Go ahead," said he.

"There are some of the foremen, and likewise some workmen, whom you know to be trustworthy. The names of a few of them probably come into your mind at once."

"Yes."

"Well, Frederic's plan is to tell them confidentially what we suspect and set them to work among the men. They in turn will know others who can be trusted. And the scheme looks good. When they realize that it's their bread and butter that's really being endangered by these insidious attempts to destroy the plant, they will rally to catch the traitors. They'll be guards as well as workmen. Their ears and eyes will be open for anything that looks suspicious; and if in time we don't lay hands on the men we want, I'm badly mistaken."

Mulhouse finished shaving his stick to a fine point. Then he tossed it down, closed his knife, looked at his watch and jerked a thumb towards the yard gate.

"It's quitting time in five minutes," he announced. "There are seven men I think of now whom we will want. I'll go round and give them a quiet word to busy themselves at something until the other fellows have gone, then to join me at the office."

"This spot here is better. No need of Andrews or Mocket knowing anything about it," said Stokes. "How long does it take the yard to empty out?"

"Fifteen or twenty minutes."

"All right. I'll be around then."

Bob returned to the office. Mocket was putting his account books in the safe. Andrews was in the inner office, helping Miss Durand seal and stamp the letters she had typed. At Stokes' entrance he showed a little confusion, but went on with his work until the envelopes were finished.

"I wasn't sure you were still here," the girl said, "so I signed the correspondence, as I've been doing heretofore. I usually take it up town, when I go, to mail in the post office."

"That's right. I didn't wish to begin on office matters until to-morrow."

Andrews stood by holding the letters, a slight cloud on his face, not looking at Stokes but conscious nevertheless of the other's gaze resting on him. The girl glanced once or twice at the pair while closing her desk, then went to a closet for her hat. Here and there along the water front whistles began to blow. The shipyard, as if by magic, ceased to resound with the noise of labor.

The girl came forward, giving a push to a pin in her hat.

"I'm ready, Mr. Andrews." Addressing Stokes, she said, "If you'll pull the door close when you go out, it will lock itself. I'll snap on the spring now. Good evening, Mr. Stokes."

"Good evening," he replied.

Andrews nodded, but did not speak. The two passed out. Stokes walked slowly to the doorway, staring whither the young fellow had followed the girl out.

"Humph," said he.

"Were you speaking to me?" Mocket inquired, turning about from giving the knob of the safe a whirl.

"No, I wasn't saying anything in particular," Bob stated.

The cashier placed his straw hat on his head, tucked away his eye-glasses in their case. His spare, black-garbed figure appeared thinner than ever.

"I hope you will find the south enjoyable, Mr. Stokes," he said, before departing. "But after a city the size of Seattle, you'll find Martinsport dull, I imagine."

"The shipyard will keep me too busy to notice it, in all probability."

"Possibly. There are few amusements, in any case."

The statement stirred a faint interest in Stokes. Mocket looked like a person whose amusements would end with a picture show and a lecture course.

The workmen were streaming out the gate when Bob stepped forth from the building. They were, on the whole, a solid, intelligent, industrious-looking body of men and supported the belief that they would respond to an appeal to aid in stamping treachery out of the plant. Strains of French, German or Scandinavian blood appeared here and there in faces that were as equally dependable as those of their fellows. Groups of lumber-handlers, roustabouts and the like—laughing and joking among themselves, made a part of the number. Altogether, the workmen formed the mixed, sturdy, honest class of toilers that constitutes the mass of loyal Americans; and at the sight Bob Stokes felt new confidence.

* * * * * * *

About eight o'clock that evening Bob approached a house on a side street in a quarter of the town where small and somewhat shabby cottages predominated. Though after sunset, it was still light. Observing the street numbers of the dwellings as he proceeded, he at last halted before one whose meager front yard was grassless and littered with the refuse of slattern housekeeping. The gate hung by a single hinge. Several dirty children squabbled and played just inside. Entering, he advanced and knocked on the door.

To his inquiry for Mr. Gaudreault a worn and untidy woman with a babe in her arms responded that her husband had just gone down town. He had just gone, she repeated. She even accompanied Bob to the gate and pointed along the street, where a man some distance away could be seen.

"That is him, see," she said. "He goes on business."

The words were uttered with extreme satisfaction.

"I can overtake him," Stokes said; and thanked her.

"You are a lawyer, eh? Perhaps about the lawsuit," she inquired, with a cunning smile. Then she turned to cuff a child who pulled at her skirt.

"Oh, no. I'm no lawyer; I only hire labor," Stokes replied.

"Jean, he is now working on Simmons' boat, shrimping." She gave a shake of her head. "No, he's not for hire this time."

"Then he can't be had?"

"No—he's shrimping."

Stokes moved away from the house at a leisurely pace, until by a look over his shoulder he perceived the woman had retired from the gate, whereupon he adopted a rapid stride. The figure of Gaudreault was three squares in advance of him, but Bob rapidly cut down the intervening space. When the woman's husband came upon the main business street, the young fellow was but a scant half-square behind. He gradually reduced the distance until the man moved only a few paces in front.

Gaudreault was short and stocky, of medium age. At one corner he loitered to exchange a word with an acquaintance, at the same time lighting a cigarette. Bob passed him and paused in a doorway. Presently, flinging a word back at his friend and showing his white teeth under his silky black mustache, the man proceeded along the street, on

which the evening crowd was idly strolling. Once
the man halted before a "movie" show, studying
the lithographs of a girl leaping from a moving
freight train; again he stopped before a glass window to adjust his tie and cock anew his vivid green
hat. But at last he entered the corridor of a six-
story office building, where as the elevators had
ceased running he began to mount the stair.

He went no higher than the first flight. Bob
heard his feet cross the hall, then came the faint
echoing sound of a knock, next the opening and
closing of a door. Three steps at a time Stokes
sprang lightly up after him. When he arrived at
the top he halted to listen. For a time he heard
nothing, but presently imagined that he distinguished muffled tones. Across from him appeared to be
a suite of rooms, apparently spacious and consti-
tuting the offices of one person at any rate, on one
door only appeared a name. It was not until the
fourth door down the hall, on that side, that other
names were in evidence.

Tiptoeing across until he stood under the open
transom of the door, he made out that two men were
talking. The speech of one was measured, com-
posed; that of the other brief and respectful—
Gaudreault's. Now and again a word or a scrap of
a sentence floated out to the hearer, but beyond perceiving that the discussion was of the lawsuit and
Gaudreault and the shipyard, Stokes was unable to
follow the talk, which was conducted at the opposite side of the room. After some fifteen minutes

he heard the speakers drawing near. Slipping along the wall, he gained the stair leading to the floor above, where he crouched in concealment.

The door opened.

"Remember carefully what you're to do, Gaudreault," said a voice.

"Yes, yes. I make no mistake."

"Then tell me," the first continued.

"Ver' well. I go to Johnson's bank and beg to borrow five hundred dollars. When I am refuse, I beg to see Mr. Johnson, who ask me why I want so much money. Then I say because I own the shipyard and will be rich. So, eh?"

"*Tres bon,* Jean. To-day is Tuesday; you will go to the bank Friday."

"And when will the lawyer get a move on him, ha?"

"Saturday, I think. He should be ready to file the suit by then. And tell your woman again not to gossip to any one of this affair, understand?"

"Yes, yes, yes!"

"When you've been to the bank, I'll advise you further. That's all for to-night. And mind, it's always the lawyer and you in this suit—never mention my name! Deny it if Johnson or any one else tries to pump you."

A laugh came from Gaudreault's lips.

"I will put it across 'em for that!" he declared.

He scuffled across the hallway and went clattering down the stair. His erstwhile companion remained unmoving, until Gaudreault's feet passed off the pavement of the corridor below, then he exclaimed, "Ye gods, what rank stuff that fellow smokes!" and reëntered the room.

Stokes lifted his head, discovering that the door had been left open. He dared not now risk a retreat. But his wait was brief; five minutes later he heard the occupant step forth, close the door behind him and go down to the street. Bob hastened after the other when assured it was safe. At the curb outside a slender gentleman with a dark striking face, wearing a Vandyke tinged with gray, was stepping into a sumptuous touring car. The negro chauffeur reaching back snapped the door shut and immediately swung the motor car out into the street.

"Who is that gentleman?" Bob asked of a policeman nearby.

"In the auto there? Broussard is his name. Owns half the town."

VII

IN THE WOODS

DARKNESS was closing down over the city as Bob Stokes made his way to the shipyard. Never one to fail to make the most of his time, especially when matters were pressing, he planned on a certain amount of night work. He needed to familiarize himself with the business details, secure at once a grasp of the main elements and features, load his head with facts. And this required a vigorous attack on the office correspondence, reports and estimates. After a tour of the yard with the head night watchman to examine the lights which had been strung about the building vessels and to inspect the arrangement of guards, he returned to the office where he plunged into work.

At about half-past ten the telephone rang in the outer office. Going to it he answered the call.

"Well, that's you, is it?" said a rough voice. "Thought I might catch you there. We're going up the line in the morning and fix those cars of lumber to-morrow night like you said, so have the rest of that money ready when we get back. And we'll collect it just the same if the cars ain't sent out, for that part's up to you."

"What's that?" Stokes demanded.

"I say we collect if they miss dropping those cars. We ain't working for nothing."

"What cars and what money are you talking about?" Bob questioned.

"Say, who's this anyway? Ain't you—— Loosen up there, who are you?"

"This is Stokes' shipyard."

"Well"—a slight pause followed—"wrong number." And the speaker abruptly hung up.

Stokes quickly rang up central and inquired who had just called. Presently he was informed the call had been made through a public pay station. So he was halted short in that direction—but he went back to his desk with the conviction that the man at the other end of the wire had lied. His tone had contained a false note; he had not had the wrong number. That being so, whom had he expected to talk with?—was it a shipment of Stokes' lumber that was concerned?—what did the fellow mean by "fix those cars"?—and who was paying money for "fixing" them? At any rate, some one in the office force was mixed up in the mysterious transaction; and the person could be only the young chap upon whom his suspicions had already centered—Andrews.

Determined to get to the bottom of the thing, he learned from Miss Durant next morning that ten cars of lumber were to be started from the mill at Hanlon fifty miles in the interior on Freight No. 15 that night. The office had been so advised by the manager of the lumber company two or three days before when he had been telephoned regarding the shipment. Mocket or Andrews usually kept after the lumber orders in order to have the material moving down regularly. Yes, she stated, there had been some delays in the past, but Mr. Stokes before he was hurt had always overcome them and made a point to keep a good supply of lumber ahead. It was necessary to have orders delivered regularly to maintain the reserve.

Bob Stokes thereupon took his hat and went to railroad headquarters, where he interviewed the division superintendent. Later in the day he went north to Hanlon on a passenger train, accompanied by a man from the superintendent's office. Occupying an hour or two there in discussion of business with the mill manager, he and his companion from Martinsport proceeded to the railway yard where Freight No. 15 lay ready to depart, located the ten cars of lumber near the forward end of the train, and then climbed aboard the caboose.

"If there's any dirty work done the train crew will have to be in on it," said the man from headquarters, whose name was Dessler. "Well, we'll know more about it before morning."

The conductor soon entered, a short grimy-faced individual, his brass badge fastened to his black slouch hat, a lantern on his arm, a lump of tobacco in his cheek.

"Can't ride with us, boys," he said briskly. "This freight doesn't carry passengers."

Dessler handed him an order. The man read it and then looked his visitors over with a trace of suspicion upon his face.

"All right; you can stretch out on these cushions," said he. "You'll find it rough going."

"Oh, we can stand it one night," Dessler answered, amicably. "Want to be on hand in town when some cotton you're carrying arrives." There were several cars of cotton in the train, as the speaker had learned. "Get there about five, don't you?"

"If we're on time."

The conductor moved away, turned and gave Stokes and Dessler a second brief inspection, appeared to be satisfied and went out.

By midnight they had passed through two towns, where a few cars were switched off and one or two picked up. At each station Dessler disappeared, rejoining Stokes only as the freight pulled out. It was as they were rumbling forward towards the third stop that a scrap of conversation between the conductor and brakeman reached Bob's ears.

"Damned funny! Something's holding up orders; don't get them till we're ready to beat it."

"Wire trouble, I reckon."

"Hasn't been any storm. Kept us waiting five minutes there at Ennis when we might have been pounding the rails."

"We can make it up at Cartersford; no work there."

"Don't you believe it!" the conductor vociferated. "Got to set ten cars out on the old switch."

The brakeman stared.

"Those cars are chalked Martinsport. Must be a mistake; there hasn't been a car run off on those streaks of rust since I can remember."

"That's where they go, just the same. Don't know why, but they do. Billed to Cartersford."

"What's the matter with you—Martinsport!"

"I'm running this train; do you get that? The scribble looks to me like Cartersford and that's what goes. Let 'em write out their orders plain if they don't want mistakes."

"Set the cars off; it's your prayer-meeting," was the unconvinced reply. "But your own sense ought to tell you they don't belong back there in the woods, where even a car accountant couldn't find 'em."

"Orders are orders," was the answer.

Stokes and Dessler, smoking and appearing oblivious to everything but the jerking of the caboose, exchanged a nudge.

Cartersford was a railway station and nothing else, a lone depot in the midst of pine woods. Perhaps there were a few shacks back in the trees, but they were not visible when Stokes followed Dessler forth upon the freight's halting. The engine was already drawing a string of cars, including Stokes' ten cars of lumber, up the track preparatory to switching work.

The two men went forward to where a dim light

showed in the depot building. Dessler made himself known to the agent.

"You have your instructions about releasing orders till I give the word?"

"Yes," said the other.

"When the crew come in asking for them, stall them off. Also wire in now for an order to pick up those cars here to be taken to Martinsport. These are the numbers. You'll receive the order immediately."

The agent glanced at the list and began to tap his key. Directly a reply was obtained.

"It's coming," said he, and seizing a pencil be began to write. Then he flung over his shoulder: "What's going on? Those cars aren't here?"

"The crew is trying to stick them on an old siding somewhere hereabouts."

"The devil they are! Are they crazy?"

Dessler and Stokes left the building. Off at their left in the night they heard the engine puffing and beheld the faint flash of its headlight through the trees.

"Now, we'll see what the rest of the play is," Dessler said. "Come along and don't get lost in the dark. I've a flash-light in my pocket, but we better not use it just yet."

Following the track they discovered the switch and made their way along in the darkness. It was not easy going, for the gloom of the woods surrounded them and the long disused roadbed, evidently at some time laid to a lumber camp, was grass-grown and rutted. When they had covered a quarter of a mile, the engine's headlight became visible. A whistle sounded.

"They're starting back. We'd better duck until they're past," Dessler said.

When the returning engine and cars had gone by, they resumed their advance. At a point two hundred yards forward Stokes uttered a low exclamation. A little way in front a lantern had moved into view.

Cautiously now they proceeded until voices came to their ears.

"Better eat our grub while we're waiting," said one. "Got to give that train time to leave."

"I don't like this so well as I did, Pete. How we goin' to get away if the timber takes fire?"

"Like we come, you fool! In the wagon. The timber won't burn much. Too wet and green."

"Well, I don't know; it's full of turpentine."

"Oh, shut up! Maybe it'll burn till the fire reaches a clearing. We'll eat and then break open these doors and pour the oil over the lumber. Soon as we touch her off, we'll head for Martinsport. Thirty miles is all; make it by daylight easy. And then we get the rest of the coin."

"Who's puttin' up for this job, Pete? You ain't never told me. Come on, spit out his name."

"Keep on guessing, for I'm not going to tell you."

"You ain't no real pal or you'd unload his name."

"Stow that. You're getting your share of the

easy money; that's enough. And there's to be more of it when this job is done."

"There won't be any more for me, for I'm going to blow north."

"Then you're a fool."

"If you're a pal and want me to stay along, hand me out this fellow's name. I'm going to know as much as you do or we split."

The discussion which had taken on an acrimonious edge promised a quarrel. The pair during their wait in the woods had been helping themselves to liquor and the second man's curiosity in consequence had settled into a stubborn insistence, interlarded as had been all their talk with oaths and curses. Stokes, on his part, was as eager to learn the men's employer as was the uninformed scoundrel.

"Well, don't make such a holler," Pete said. "I'm holdin' nothing out on you. We've been pals a long time, Jack, and we won't quit on account of this feller's name. His name is Smith."

"Is that straight, Pete? Smith ain't no name; it's just a label. Too many Smiths for that."

"He says his name is Smith and I asks no questions. His money is what talks with me.

Stokes' keen anticipation evaporated in disappointment. He had hoped to learn to a certainty the man instigating the subtle attacks upon his company. If Smith were really the congnomen of the chief plotter, then the man was a stranger. But if, as he guessed, it was but an alibi, he still was none the wiser.

The two disreputables, continuing their talk, went with their lantern to a spot on one side of the track, where sitting upon the ground they produced a bottle, had a drink apiece and opened a package of food.

"Do you recognize one of those fellows as the man who called your office by telephone?" Dessler asked of Stokes.

"That man named Pete."

"You'll now run down the traitor in your employ, of course. That is up to you. Meanwhile we'll grab these chaps. Steal up on them quietly till we're near enough to cover them with our guns. This isn't only your game remember, but the railroad's as well; they plan to destroy our cars along with your lumber. It will be the pen for them!"

Using stealth in their advance towards the pair of criminals, Stokes and Dessler proceeded until from a nearby bush they had a dim view of Pete and Jack and again could hear their rough talk. Close at hand and shining dully in the lantern's light were three square, tin, ten-gallon cans of oil, with which the men proposed to spray the cars and fire them. Where were tied the horses and wagon in which the hirelings had come, the observers could only guess, for neither animals nor vehicle were visible; no doubt, somewhere not far off in the darkness.

Pete and Jack ate and conversed and grunted and

occasionally washed their throats with a draught of whiskey.

"Well, that train hasn't gone yet," the latter was saying.

"They'll be pullin' along by the time we're done eatin'." the other answered. "Unloadin' some stuff, maybe."

"Wonder how much the crew got for their end of this job."

"Don't know and don't care. We'll get what's comin' to us; that's all I'm interested in, bo." A wave of a dirty hand emphasized his indifference to extraneous matters.

At this instant Dessler touched Stokes' arm warningly. The two listeners thereupon noiselessly stepped round their bush near to the seated men.

"Take a look at this and see how it interests you," Dessler said to the speaker.

With a start Pete jerked his face about towards the voice. What he saw appeared to interest him considerably. It was the muzzle of a revolver leveled at his eyes.

VIII

FIRST BLOOD

"Huh," escaped Pete's lips.

"Stick your fins up," was Dessler's command.

Reluctantly Pete's hands went above his head, as did his companion's. But the men's surprise was only momentary; their faces grew vicious as they realized that they had been nabbed when they fancied themselves in greatest security.

At Dessler's further order they got to their feet, while Bob Stokes searched them, removing a pistol from the hip pocket of each man. During the procedure the prisoners exchanged furtive glances, though saying nothing.

"Take the lantern," Dessler said to Stokes, "and lead the way with them, while I keep my gun on their backs."

Bob stooped to lift the light. Like a flash Pete seized his shoulders, swung him about as a shield, gave a swift kick at the lantern that extinguished it and shattered its globe of glass. Impenetrable darkness shrouded the spot. A sound of running feet, at which Dessler fired once, twice, was heard— the sound of the second man, Jack, fleeing away in the wood.

With Pete, Stokes was rolling on the earth in a fierce hand to hand struggle. When Bob had felt his shoulders caught, he instantly flung his arms about the other's waist and hurled him down. Over and over on the pine mold they threshed, the man beating at Bob's head and trying to break his bear-hug, while Stokes squeezed his antagonist's body with arms hardened by toil in woods and lumber camps to the strength of iron.

At last he had the savage scoundrel Pete's back upon the ground, where squirm as the man would he could not get free. Their breathings were audible to Dessler, who listened unable to distinguish their forms or to render assistance. Suddenly Bob slipped a hand out and dealt Pete a frightful smash in the face. A groan, a relaxing of the man's body, a stilling of his struggles, was the result.

"Light a match," Bob said.

Quickly Dessler did so, bending down and holding the flame close over Pete's face. A dark trickle of blood ran from one nostril out over his cheek. The prostrate figure groaned, moved, became quiet again.

"Good work," Dessler stated. "You knocked him out; he ought to be good now."

Stokes hoisted himself off his opponent, got on one knee. The match flickered and died down to a coal between Dessler's fingers. As this happened, Pete groaned a third time. Then an oath exploded in his mouth. He whirled himself from beneath Bob's fingers resting on his chest and rolled noisily from the spot into a bush, tore himself out again while gaining his feet, eluded the men who had rushed at him and fled. Dessler could only shoot where he thought Pete might be, as he had done with the other scoundrel,—futile shots.

"Clumsy work on our part," he said to Stokes, in disgust. "No use trying to find them now. We didn't even get a good look at their faces, dim as that lantern was. Could you identify the pair if you saw them later?"

"I doubt it—unless by their voices."

"Well, we saved the cars any way; we'll pour out this oil. Listen! They're signaling each other."

Off in the darkness they heard low quick whistles, then guarded calls.

"We've their guns and their oil, so their teeth have been drawn," Stokes said. "And they'll no more know us by the glimpse they had than we'll know them. Very likely they'll lead their horses and wagon to a road and make the dust fly for town."

"I'll send a wire through to headquarters to have the police on the lookout for them," Dessler stated. "But I imagine they will leave the wagon on the outskirts and sneak in. They will be aware that we're trying to head them off. Now we'll spill this oil and go to the depot. Those fellows won't come back, never fear, knowing we're about."

The oil disposed of, Stokes and Dessler retraced their way along the old railway track until they came again to where the freight stood. The engine's

great beam illuminated the space in front; steam
was hissing in the locomotive's valves; but the train
waited.

Why it waited was apparent when the two men
entered the depot. There the conductor and brakeman and engineer were fretting because of the unreasonable delay.

"All right, give 'em that late order," Dessler said
to the agent, who immediately handed it forth to
the conductor.

"You been sitting here with orders all the time?"
that worthy shouted, "while we had to stand round
waiting?"

"Sure. Couldn't give them to you until Mr. Dessler said so."

The engineer turned angrily on Dessler.

"What have you got to do with it? Damned
queer if this train can't start till a passenger gives
the word. I'll have something to say when I get
to headquarters."

"You'll have a good deal to say and to explain;
you're right about that," was the answer. "Now
read that order, then go pick up those ten cars you
hid back there in the timber."

The conductor glared incredulously. Finally he
examined the order and his grimy face grew dark.

"Who faked this?" he demanded of the agent.

"That's a straight order and you better get busy.
I've instructions to report those cars out of here."

"And I'm present to see that they do go out,"
Dessler said, thrusting his jaw close to the con-

ductor's face. "What's more, if you don't pull them out of that brush back there at once I'll discharge you, hand the train over to the brakeman and take you into Martinsport under arrest."

The conductor began to moisten his lips.

"Say, what's the matter with you! I'm going to get them. But my original orders said they were to be shunted off here at——"

"You're a liar. You were paid to hide them in there. When we get to Martinsport we're going to sweat you till you come across with the man's name who is paying you too, you crook."

"Nobody's paying me. It was a mistake, it was a mistake in the orders," the conductor declared, regaining his assurance. "You can sweat me for a month of Sundays, and fire me too, and I'll tell your whole bunch of officials you can't make me the goat for somebody else's mistake."

"Go get those cars," Dessler ordered.

The conductor who was about to speak again, closed his lips, swung about and followed by brakeman and engineer went out.

"Give them the rest of the orders," Dessler told the agent, "when they come back. You can wire in that we're on our way when you see our tail lights."

On the platform outside he and Stokes kept watch until the engine's headlight once more broke into view, returning from the wood. When it backed down on the main track and the men had by a personal count assured themselves as to the cars, they footed it to the caboose.

"Dessler, I'm going to take you into my confidence," Bob Stokes remarked. "To-night's affair is part of a scheme to put our company out of business. My brother's injury, of which you've perhaps heard, was likewise a part of the secret attack. Some one is employing thugs, corrupting our workmen, harassing our yard. We don't know who, but we intend to find out."

"I should think so!"

"You'll probably discover that this conductor will stick to his claim of a mistake and as long as we can't produce the men who were to have destroyed the lumber and cars, our story won't amount to much in proving his connection. Probably he knew nothing of what was to be done when the cars were set off on that blind switch. The chief plotter alone holds all the strings, I imagine. If this fellow should be forced to confess, which I doubt will happen, as he's a sullen brute and unquestionably well paid, we'd hear that his employer was 'Smith' as before."

"Yes," Dessler replied, with a nod.

"The men higher up are keeping concealed," Stokes went on. "But we have suspicions. There are five men in Martinsport called the Big Five—you've heard of them."

"Heard of them? Who hasn't! I know them all. Great heavens, Stokes, you don't mean to tell me you believe these men are at the bottom of this villainous plot against your concern? No, no; I'll never think that! They're sharp business men, but respected. They would never risk their position—good Lord, no!"

"I don't say they're responsible. But the two bankers are interested in our affairs, and all five of the men tried to force us to let them into our business. This man Main, one of them——"

"'Gas' Main, yes," Dessler interrupted. "He's the one hard customer in the Big Five. He likes to use a club; he imported a lot of strike-breakers here during the street car strike last summer, who beat up the local workmen pretty badly. He would go far to have his way. But still—no, I put this sort of work past even him."

"Well, Main and Derland have nothing to do with this assault on us, as far as I know," Stokes said. "They've displayed no interest in the business. I only suspect that the bankers would like to squeeze us; and I don't believe they would try to shanghai our shipyard criminally, from what I've been advised. What, however, of the other fellow, Broussard?"

"Broussard is as rich as sin, but he has a reputation for being a good fellow and liberal to the poor. In fact, I know of poor families he has helped. Stokes, I can't credit any man of the Big Five engaged in a job like to-night's. Not a one of them would condescend to exchange two words with ruffians such as we routed out yonder."

Stokes smote a fist upon his knee.

"Just the same, this Broussard is setting an ignorant Frenchman to suing us in the hope of tying our

yard up by an injunction. That's as bad as burning our lumber or hitting us behind the ear with a
rock; worse, in fact."

"Still it's not the same. It's only legal sharp
practice."

"Of those five men, this Broussard I know is
fighting us. I merely surmise that Johnson and Farrington, from what my brother tells me, may be in
the game; but they haven't disclosed their hand if
they are. Main and Derland I count out of it altogether. But all five of the clique may be associated
in the raid."

"They frequently work together on a big deal,"
Dessler said. "But, no. This criminal affair isn't
in their line. Main would use any means in a fight,
for he's built that way—a business ruffian. But he
has sense too. And the rest wouldn't let him get
out of bounds. Why, Johnson and Farrington are
church pillars."

"Fond of money, though, I've heard," was Bob's
dry comment. "Some of the worst money-tigers
I ever saw cover their backs and financial operations
with a respectable church mantle."

"Well, I'll stake my head you'll discover some
one else is the author of these dangerous attempts
against your firm."

"What would be the motive? German spy work?
No. It would not be limited to our ten cars of lumber if it were. An effort would be made to destroy
the whole train and generally wreck your railroad
service. Nothing to that. I can't figure out any

reason whatever why any outsider—apart from the five men mentioned, I mean—should have a reason for putting us on the rocks."

Dessler shook his head.

"Nor can I, but such you will learn probably is the case."

"One line is left me," Stokes said grimly.

"What is that?"

"The yellow-hearted scoundrel in our office who's selling us out. I've my eye on the man now, I think. I'll continue to give him more rope till I have him wound up good and tight; then I'll grab him by the throat. Of all traitors the worst is the fellow who takes your money and at the same time betrays you to an enemy! There will be no mercy from Stokes Brothers, believe me, once we catch this knave for sure. And through him we'll land the man or men who are profiting from his disloyalty."

The train had already started from the station by now, and the conductor and brakeman at this moment entering the car the discussion ceased. The former glared at the two passengers with a bellicose aspect that indicated he would be pleased to slay them on the cushions where they sat. But looks do not kill.

"I thought you guys were 'spotters' when you first got aboard up the line," he sneered. "I'd take a smash at you for two-bits."

Bob Stokes bounded to his feet.

"I'm aching for you to try it, you thief!" he exclaimed. "You have the dirty money in your pocket this minute, I'm betting, that you took for sticking my cars of lumber on that rusty switch where they wouldn't be found for a month."

"Here's where you eat those words," the other snarled. "No dressed up dude can give me that kind of talk without getting a come-back." And he promptly hung his lantern on a hook.

Evidently he believed Stokes to be a dude. Though somewhat rumpled from his earlier struggle, Bob's light gray suit, white shoes and linen led the freight conductor to imagine he had found an easy victim on whom to vent his accumulated rage. He faced a discharge at Martinsport, at least, for which his ill-gotten gains would but partly compensate; he boiled to beat one or both of the men who had detected him in his deception.

On his part, Bob Stokes was no less eager to satisfy an ardent longing for action, whetted by the escape of the hirelings in the woods and by his failure to learn the instigator of the plot. For a few dollars the man before him had sold out his trust and his honor, if he ever had such. For a few dollars he had been ready to do his share to cripple the shipyard. And beyond "firing" him the railroad would be able to do nothing. He deserved more punishment and Bob was determined he should have it.

The young brakeman in affright backed away from the spot, taking refuge at the end of the car.

Dessler glanced at Stokes, shrewdly smiled, and slipped away towards the door.

A quick jab at Stokes was the trainman's opening. "Your face won't be so pretty when I'm done molding it," he grated, with an oath.

Bob retreated slightly. Then like a flash he leaned forward and tapped the other on the nose with a sharp blow. The man blinked for an instant, after which a dark wave of blood surged into his grimy face. His lips curled back from his teeth exactly in the manner of a wild animal.

With a sudden rush he launched himself at Stokes, raining swinging blows that the young fellow stopped with his guard. In the narrow space between the two long seats there was no room to sidestep or circle about. But Stokes was the taller and had the longer reach, and in addition had not boxed in a Seattle athletic club to no avail. In an opening he swung a short uppercut to the man's jaw that sent his head back with a jerk, then followed it by a lively jolt on the solar plexus.

"What led you to think you could fight?" Stokes asked, as the fellow stood in distress, his face turning pale beneath its coating of coal-dust.

Into the eyes of the man came a murderous gleam. Hurling himself forward he struck madly at the young fellow, cursing and snapping, kicking with his heavy shoes. The rocking, jerking motion of the car flung the pair together. Instantly the man was clawing at Stokes' face, but the latter shoved him back.

"I'll tear your black heart out!" the man howled, launching himself anew.

Stokes crouched, swiftly beat down the other's flailing blows. Then with a step ahead he shot his fist to his assailant's jaw in a sledge-hammer crash that tumbled the other against the side of the car, whence he slumped to the cushion and from that to the aisle floor. There the fellow squirmed until he had supported his figure on one hand, striving through a mist to distinguish Stokes. His face worked in a hideous grimace. With his free hand he endeavored to drag a revolver from his pocket.

"Grab that gun!" Stokes commanded sharply, to the brakeman.

Tremulously the youth advanced, pulled it from the fallen man's fingers, loosed it from the pocket, retired again. All at once the defeated fighter sank and lay unconscious.

Once more Stokes addressed the brakeman.

"Give me that pistol and throw a bucket of water over his head. That will bring him around. And you better take charge of the train—eh, Dessler?"

"Yes," said Dessler. "And I've certainly enjoyed our ride to-night, Stokes."

IX

MR. BROUSSARD TURNS THE OTHER CHEEK

On Thursday morning of that week Mr. Willard, who had returned from the north, had a conference with the two Stokes at the bed-side of the injured member of the firm. It appeared that John Stokes had been in telegraphic communication with him from Seattle. Afterwards Mr. Willard and Bob went to an attorney's office, with the result that that afternoon a mortgage for four hundred thousand dollars, blanketing the two vessels under construction and made to the Willard Pacific Coast Development Company, was placed on record at the county recorder's office. Then the attorney made a point of dropping in to consult Johnson, the banker, on a matter of minor business.

"By the way, how's Stokes Brothers' credit?" he inquired, as he was leaving.

"Good. Why?" was Johnson's response.

"Oh, nothing especial. I filed a big mortgage for them to-day. Wondered if they were sailing close to the wind."

When he was back in his office again, he telephoned Bob.

"Just saw your man," said he. "Let out a word of the transaction, as you wished."

"Much obliged. I'll run in and see you to-morrow or next day. I'll advise with you when Gaudreault's suit starts," Bob stated. "I should learn something from the banker presently."

Nor had he long to wait. Five minutes later the telephone rang again. The speaker, naming himself as Mr. Johnson, requested him to meet Mr. Farrington and himself at ten o'clock on the following morning if convenient. They wished to discuss the matter of Stokes Brothers' loan. Bob assured him it would be convenient.

Towards five o'clock that afternoon a colloquy in the outer office drew the young fellow thither. A man not less than six feet two in height, rawboned and weather-beaten, with a dirty white cap that advertised somebody's lumber stuck on one side of his head, and wearing bibbed overalls, was informing Mocket that he was a carpenter looking for a job. He did not appear to impress the spare ascetic cashier favorably. The stranger talked in a loud voice. His huge curved nose, bent in some fist fight, and his wide mouth that shut askew with a trap-like assertiveness when he ceased speaking could not be called handsome. As he stated his qualifications, which included an ability to build anything from a canoe to a battleship, he leaned an elbow familiarly on the counter and waved before the other a hand like a slab of mahogany.

"The superintendent employs the carpenters," Mocket stated.

"Well, trot him out, brother," the stranger replied.

"You'll find him in the yard somewhere."

The other struck a match on his bib and lighted a short, villainous-smelling pipe.

"Well, where? I don't want to be cruising all over the place, kicking niggers out of my way."

"At one of the ships, very likely," was the disdainful answer.

"All right, boy. And farewell till I come fluttering in for my pay check. Try eating more to fatten yourself up."

He lifted a sack of tools from the floor and swung it over his shoulder. Next his eyes encountered Bob. A faint grin rested on his lips as he stared at the young fellow for the space of a minute, then he swung about towards the door.

"Wait till I get my hat," Bob said. "I'm going to see the superintendent and I'll take you along."

As the pair left the office, Mocket exclaimed something half aloud that made Andrews glance at him quickly. The word was spoken unconsciously, contemptuously, in another tongue. But when the cashier moved about to resume his work the youth in the pink shirt and flamboyant tie was industriously writing. Mocket had caught himself up after the utterance, and now regarded Andrews sharply, who continued absorbed as if unaware of the other's gaze.

Outside Bob Stokes and the giant moved away from the door. When they were out of ear-shot, the latter said:

"How's tricks, Bob?"

"Pretty fair, old scout. Come through all right, I see."

"Oh, yes. Tangled with a couple of bar-room comrades in Saint Louis, who wanted my bank-roll. One wallop apiece put 'em to sleep under the table like slumbering infants, Bob, and then I went out the side door to the station, while the bar-keep was rounding up a cop. Mussed up his place some. What's doing here?"

Stokes enlightened his companion as to the nature of the business on hand. Snohomish Jim was to discover if possible and associate himself with the men who were causing accidents in the ship-yards, in fact, he was to become one of them. Bob would supply him with money and Jim should choose his own devices.

"Leave it to me, Bob. This is a dry town, but there's boot-leggers a-plenty I heard coming in on the train," was Snohomish Jim's assuring answer. "I'll get next to these ship-scuttlers and load 'em with pine-juice till they tell their life histories on my bosom. Never saw a crook yet who didn't fall for booze."

"When you get to sizing up the workmen," Bob said, "observe whether or not they have a piece of blue string tied to their suspenders or to a button anywhere. If they have, count them out. We are lining up the men to be trusted and letting them know the state of affairs, so they can be on the lookout for crooked work also. The men with the bits of string are O. K. We started with seven night before last, and got twenty more last night whom the first bunch vouched for. They're feeling out others and we'll probably add another and bigger crowd to the number this evening, keeping on with the plan every day until we have nearly the whole force with us."

"That will scale my job down considerable," Jim remarked. "And I reckon you don't want me wearing any string."

"No, I'll give Mulhouse, the superintendent, to understand what you're about. The others will probably come to suspect you, but so much the better."

Jim grinned, then expectorated.

"They'll surely think me a low-browed dynamite artist before I'm through," said he.

Half an hour later Snohomish Jim was smoothing a ship rib with an adze and relating to two companion workers on the scaffold a tale that never happened on land or sea. It was a story of the blowing up of a mine shaft in the mountains when a strike was on, and where Jim purported to have been a mine carpenter temporarily. Jim declared it was the fault of the capitalists. He denounced capitalists in general. And during the next few days, as he was systematically shifted about by Mulhouse, now working in one gang and now in another, he breathed the same hatred for men of wealth. He was an I. W. W., he asserted, and didn't care who knew it.

On Friday morning, prompt to the minute, Stokes appeared in the Marine Exchange Bank and making himself known was conducted into the president's private office. There Johnson and Farrington awaited him. He had met neither gentlemen, but was able at first glance to identify each by the description of them he had received from his brother. Mr. Johnson introduced himself, then Farrington, who scrutinized the young visitor with frowning gravity. When Bob was seated, the president of the Marine Exchange opened up.

"As you, of course, are aware, Mr. Stokes, Mr. Farrington and I have made a loan of a considerable amount to your company." He placed the tips of his fingers together as he spoke while gently rocking back and forth in his swivel chair. "So naturally the affairs of your concern interest us. We've learned that you have placed a heavy mortgage upon the ships that you're building."

"Quite right," said Bob.

"How does that affect the notes we hold?"

"Well, how does it?" Stokes demanded.

"Presuming that the mortgage is foreclosed——"

"Oh, it will not be foreclosed. We'll take care of it and the notes also. And anyway, you're secured."

"If the mortgage should take the boats," Johnson persisted, "what's the security worth? Have you

other money to pay us? And what will be done with
the money raised on the mortgage!"

Bob smiled.

"There isn't any money from the mortgage,"
said he. "It covers past expenditures for lumber
mostly, though we have a hundred thousand dollars
credit now out of it. One of Mr. Willard's companies is to supply us with material to that amount.
That will go into our second vessel. You see, out
of the two hundred thousand borrowed of you gentlemen, about half went into paying back money
used to buy the grounds and build ways and so on.
while the rest has been used for our wage roll.
Then to take care of material accounts, additional
labor expenses and the like, we placed the mortgage
on the boats. Of course, if anything happened to
delay completion of the boats before the mortgage
matured—it's a short-time mortgage—we should be
kept busy scratching. We'll have to find some
more money somewhere as it is, very likely,
before we launch our first boat. Our chief trouble
at present is with delays and labor difficulties, which
are throwing us behind schedule. But we'll pull
through. Those two ships will bring a million when
ready to sail. Oh, yes, we'll have plenty of money
then!"

"But if you don't and Willard takes them, Stokes
Brothers will have only its shipyard?"

"Worth a hundred thousand only, if that!" Farrington interjected, sharply. "And your company
is capitalized for half a million!"

Stokes nodded to the statement.

"We decided half a million was enough," he remarked.

"Enough! On a property worth only one-fifth of the amount!" the little man cried, clawing his chin whisker and glaring at the speaker. "This is a swindle if there ever was one. The collateral we hold, figured at its best, represents only fifty thousand dollars. Do you hear that, Johnson? We don't even have all the stock; this Stokes outfit kept the other half."

Raising a propitiatory hand Bob brought the little financier to silence, though the latter continued to twitch and fume and glare.

"I fear you are too pessimistic as to our ability to work out from under our obligations," said the visitor.

Johnson stood on his feet. His face had slowly grown pink and now he shook a stern finger at his visitor.

"Young man, I want to say that the members of your firm are started on a course that will lead them behind the bars," he announced. "You've floated this concern on air: your brother led us to believe it was sound when it was not; you've mismanaged the business; you've allowed your workmen to injure the property——"

"Are you responsible for that?" Bob demanded, suddenly, leaning across the table and in turn pointing a finger at the bank president. "Because it looks like it. You're the only parties interested in our success or failure. Wouldn't you two men have liked to gobble up our business? What has been happening in our yard is the result of deliberate plotting to ruin us, the delays, the accidents, the interference with work, and it began immediately after you made the loan to us. We're going to nab the men you've employed and squeeze the truth out of them, and then you'll have a damage suit on your hands that will make you take notice, to say nothing of the stench it will raise in the town. My brother was injured maliciously. And I think you two schemers hired the man who did the trick. Don't talk to me about going behind bars! We'll have a confession from some one one of these days that will make you feel sick. We're after you and we're going to get you. I'm through now, and going. You can't hand that kind of talk to me and get away with it."

"You lying young wretch!" Farrington squealed, springing up. "We're not responsible for what's happened in your yard, if anything crooked has happened!"

"The court will decide that—and your dirty tactics will get a fine airing, believe me. You can't send an assassin to kill my brother and not suffer for it. Wait till we spring that confession on the public!" And seizing his hat Bob Stokes strode out of the office, convinced that even if the men were not implicated the shaking down he had given them had done no harm.

Johnson still remained transfixed, his finger pointing where Stokes had been when he addressed him. Farrington champed his jaws in rage.

"Did you hear the young scoundrel?" he exclaimed, finally.

"I did—it was outrageous, infamous!" Johnson responded. Then he lowered his hand at a new thought. "This is the first I've heard of any plot. But I recall now that there's been talk of accidents and so on at the yard, and there's the injury of this chap's brother? Could it be possible that some one's been causing their trouble deliberately, as he says?"

"We certainly didn't," Farrington snapped.

"But he seems to think we did. If they started a damage suit against us on the evidence of some lying workman, even if they lost the case, it would be very unpleasant, very unpleasant indeed. I should not care to be brought into court to deny an allegation to the effect of employing men to injure Stokes Brothers' plant and to murder one of the firm. Would you?"

"Of course not!"

"I fear, Farrington, we're in a nasty affair."

"Nonsense," said the other, but less vigorously.

"And it looks as if the loan itself is bad."

"It's worse than bad, it's rotten," Farrington responded. "I thought I was too old to be jig-sawed in any such fashion. They're going to trim us, if we're not careful." He leaned an elbow on the table and covered his eyes with a hand. "I have a feeling that old man Willard is pulling on the line and hook too—the mortgage was made to him and from what

I've learned he's been friendly with these Stokes."

"Then you don't think the company is broke?" Johnson asked.

"Don't talk that way; you give me a headache. To be sure, it's not broke. Didn't we look up its rating out west? Willard will take over the ships and then they'll be finished and sold and they'll split the clean-up between them. And we'll have paid two hundred thousand for a half interest in a ship-yard worth one hundred thousand. Don't interrupt me again with foolish questions; I want to think."

Johnson allowed his associate to think. He was also trying to think of something himself, but not successfully. The prospect of realizing twenty-five cents on the dollar when he had expected to realize a dollar from twenty-five cents was so utterly at variance with the customary results of his operations that his brain suffered a sort of numbness. His mind failed to spark, as it were.

It was at this point that a clerk appeared and announced a new visitor. Ordinarily Johnson would have made inquiries concerning his business, but now he absently ordered the man to be admitted. Gaudreault, twisting his green hat and smiling ingratiatingly, entered.

"Mr. Johnson will consider your request," the clerk informed his charge and then vanished.

"What is it?" Johnson asked, bending his eyes on the man.

"I beg to borrow five hundred dollars."

"The cashier would have attended to you. What security?"

"I have no security, no, but I am to be rich nex' week, very rich. So I mus' have the money," Gaudreault stated, modestly.

"What are you going to do with the money?"

"To make ready to be rich. For the clothes, for the lawyer, for many things."

Johnson frowned at the fellow.

"I don't know what you're talking about, but what's this of your going to be rich?" he demanded.

"It is nex' week. Nex' week I will have the shipyard. The lawyer begins a lawsuit to get it for me, because the ground belongs to me and not to this Stokes company. The company will be put off by what the lawyer calls injunction. Ships all tied up. Work all stopped. Gates all locked. Nothing doing. I, Gaudreault, will own it, because I am heir way back from my family. So I mus' have five hundred dollars."

Farrington came swiftly round the table. He seized the little fisherman by the coat lapel and shook him.

"Who's your lawyer?" he barked.

"Mr. Guyenne."

Dropping his hand, the banker seated himself at Johnson's desk, called central to give him Guyenne's office without troubling to look up the number and fidgeted till he had the connection. Then he shot a number of rapid questions into the receiver concerning Gaudreault and the shipyard and the lawsuit. Finally he jabbed the receiver back on its hook.

"Well, it's to be started," he informed Johnson. "Get rid of this fellow."

"We don't loan money on the strength of lawsuits," Gaudreault was informed.

Gaudreault went out.

When Johnson turned about, his companion was pinching his lip and meditating. His air nevertheless was peevish, so that it did not appear wise at the moment to question him further concerning the lawsuit. At all times irritable, Farrington was not sweetened by the disclosures of the morning.

"Who shall we unload on?" he asked at last. "We can't send the paper out of town because we should have to guarantee it, and when we sell we shall sell without recourse, of course. We can't split the loan up unfortunately, as it's one note."

"Well, you know who can take a note of that size," Johnson stated, significantly. "And there's no one else who's able. But you remember what Main said if he learned we were cutting him and Derland out of any transaction with the Stokes."

"I remember."

For half an hour they discussed the matter without deciding on a definite course. At the end of that time Johnson was called out of the room on a matter of business. He beheld Broussard seated inside the railing, engaged in discussion with the cashier. When a moment later Johnson returned Broussard thanked the cashier for the information obtained and arose.

"How about a round of nine holes about four o'clock?" he inquired of the bank president. "Time you were cutting down that adipose."

"Can't do it to-day, Broussard," Johnson replied. "Too busy."

"You're a good bluffer. Well, I'm thinking of running up to New York, so if I'm not at the gas company meeting you'll know why—and don't slip anything over on me while I'm away from it. I've some loose money and thought I'd go up to Wall Street and pick up a few stocks."

Broussard smiled lazily with his full black eyes fixed on the other as if amused at something. All at once Johnson caught him by the arm.

"Come in with me a moment," he said.

"There you go. The minute I say money, you want to try and sell me a gold brick, Johnson. What do you imagine you can work off on me now?"

But Broussard nevertheless accompanied the bank president into his sanctum. Farrington stared at the new comer without any sign of friendliness on his face, until Johnson gave him a significant nod. Then the frost died out of his countenance.

"Well, well, well, the vultures have cornered the lamb," Broussard remarked, when the door was closed and he had dropped into a seat. "I'm afraid I gave myself away when I told you, Johnson, that I had some loose change. Now go to it. I'll wager you two want to dump that West Avenue sub-division off on me."

"No, we've only got a piece of first-class paper to sell, amply secured."

"Show me the stuff," said Broussard, "I can tell you in one minute whether I'd touch it at all and tell you in two what I'll give for it."

His indolent air had been dispelled in an instant and he was now alert, watchful.

"It's a Stokes Brothers' note for two hundred thousand dollars, secured by two hundred and fifty of stock, half the capitalization," Johnson stated.

"What's wrong with the company?"

"Nothing, sound as a bell," Farrington put in. "But we need cash for a bunch of houses we want to erect out on the avenue. We've looked up Stokes Brothers and they're rated high. I can show you the reports at my bank."

"Never mind them. Let me have a look at this note and the stock."

Johnson touched a bell. Presently a clerk appeared in answer to the summons. He was directed to bring the president's private file of notes. When it was delivered, Johnson ran through the pockets, selected an envelope and extracted the note and collateral. He tossed them over to Broussard.

The latter inspected them. Then drew out a check book and made out a check. He handed it to Farrington.

"One hundred and seventy-five thousand dollars!" the latter yelped. "What do you mean? What

do you think we are? Of all damnable insolence!
No interest figured and twenty-five thousand under
the face!"

Lighting a cigarette, Broussard exhaled a puff towards the ceiling.

"Take it or leave it; that's my offer," said he.
"You're eager to let go of the paper for some reason, or you wouldn't sell it at all. Your story of
building houses is moonshine. I'm buying blind,
but I'm willing to take a chance. It has to be a
bargain, or we don't do business—I'm not taking the
note for amusement. I like to see a profit right on
the jump. Twenty-five thousand isn't any too much
to charge for letting you fellows unload. Take it or
leave it, that's my last word."

Johnson protested hotly. Farrington snapped
forth his opinion of Broussard in a hundred biting
expressions. But the latter only smoked and smiled
and from time to time glanced at his watch.

"Well, I see we're not going to make a deal," he
stated finally, rising. "Give me that check and I'll
tear it up."

But Farrington continued to hold it in his fingers.

"You'd rob a beggar if you got a chance!" he
snarled. Then, turning to Johnson, he continued,
"You can't squeeze blood out of a turnip. Turn in
this check while I'm putting my endorsement on the
note—I wouldn't put it past him to stop payment if
he should decide to buck back on the deal."

Broussard smiled down his nose. Johnson went

out with the check, as suggested. Farrington scribbled his name on the note with a pen.

"No recourse," he bit forth.

"Rest easy; I know better than to ask it," was the
reply.

When the bank president returned, he added his
name to the note and passed it over, together with
the collateral, to Broussard. Then he and Farrington began to smile.

"Hee, hee, you've bought something this time!"
the latter exclaimed, with sudden glee. "For your
information I'll say the Stokes concern mortgaged
both their ships to the last stick yesterday, somebody's raising the devil with their yard and they're
about to be sued by claimants of the ground and
tied up tighter than a bale of cotton by an injunction. This collateral stock is worth maybe fifty
thousand, maybe twenty-five, maybe nothing when
the lawsuit's ended. Hee, hee!"

"Yes, you've bought something," Johnson agreed,
complacently.

Broussard regarded them with a cold eye.

"I learned of the mortgage this morning; it does-
n't disturb me," he remarked. "Don't exult, for the
Stokes will take care of it—I'll see to that. And I
imagine the person or persons who're responsible
for their yard trouble, if troubles there have been,
will also be disposed of. So don't sympathize with
me too soon."

But Farrington did not lose his malicious grin.

"There's the lawsuit," he exclaimed. "That will

tie the yard up till not a hammer is lifted. The men will be laid off. The boats will remain where they are, unfinished. And if the Stokes Company loses, it'll not have even the ground. We'll teach you to try to lift twenty-five thousand dollars out of our wallets! You thought you were getting your hooks into us! This makes me feel better than anything that's happened in a year."

Placing the note and stock certificate in his pocket, Broussard walked to the telephone and called for a number.

"Nothing is more admirable than an old gentleman happy and serene in the knowledge he has lived a useful, unselfish life," he remarked at large, as he waited on central. Then immediately he spoke into the mouth-piece of the telephone, "This you, Guyenne? Broussard speaking. You have Gaudreault there? Well, you can tell him now that the evidence doesn't justify a suit after all. Pay him five hundred and let him go. Yes, that's all." Broussard replaced the receiver upon its hook.

Farrington was on his feet, shaking a hand furiously at the other.

"You framed this lawsuit, you framed it to skin us!" he shrieked, in a splutter of sounds. "You thief, you robber—you——"

"Outrageous, infamous!" Johnson cried, angrily.

A satirical smile rested on Broussard's lips as he picked up his hat and walking-stick. Sauntering towards the door, he sang:

"You say the time has come to part, my dear-ie!
You say our love was never meant to last!—
And with your words the world grows dark and drear,
Transformed from sunshine of the past."

X

THE OBSCURE FACTOR

MR. MOCKET, the tall, thin and serious-faced cashier of Stokes Brothers, had occasion to transact some business at the Marine Exchange Bank that morning towards noon. As he entered the building, Broussard was just departing after his successful crossing of swords with the two bankers in Johnson's private office. Broussard turned to look after Mocket's spare, erect figure.

"Wonder what that fellow's doing since he stopped handling Main's crooked work for him?" he asked himself.

Broussard had a faculty of discovering considerable more of his financial associates' affairs than Main, Derland, Johnson and Farrington suspected. He was aware for instance that Mocket at one time while ostensibly a clerk in Main's employ had in fact managed such discreditable business as the gas magnate wanted put through but in which he did not wish personally to appear. And he had learned too that the man for some reason had been discharged by Main.

However, his curiosity concerning the fellow was but momentary and he immediately continued on his way. Mocket, on his part, concluded his bank business and thereupon proceeded not to the ship-yard but to the building where his former employer, Main, held forth. There he was admitted into the presence of the financier.

The burden of his errand had to do with expense money, it appeared, as after a brief remark that progress in a certain affair was being made he stated that he should need two hundred dollars.

"I pay for what I get, but I want to know that I'm actually getting value received when I do pay," Main stated, bluntly, and in a tone that made the other's lips tighten. "What have you accomplished?"

"Do you want the details?"

Main, with his heavy jowls spreading over the edge of his collar, stared stonily at his secret employee.

"No, I've told you before I don't care to be bothered with the details, don't care to know anything about them. I wash my hands of them—but I want results!"

"You are getting results, Mr. Main."

"Well, what?"

"In delayed work. You said in the beginning that delay would be the one thing which would bring pressure to bear to accomplish the financial end you had in view. I don't know what that end is, but if you would take me into your confidence to a further degree I perhaps should be able to proceed more effectively."

"Never you mind what my game is," Main exclaimed, truculently. "You do what you're ordered; that's enough for you. I don't trust you more than from here to the shipyard and besides I can get along without your financial advice. I've got you where I want you, so you'll do exactly as I say unless you want to wear stripes. When I have a man under my hand, he works as I tell him to work or I smash him."

At the insolent brutal words the thin spare figure quivered. Behind the glasses Mocket wore his eyes flashed in a single murderous gleam, then again became vague and expressionless.

"I shall remember, sir," said he, quietly.

"You had better remember, for it isn't too late yet to dig up the proof on that embezzlement charge if I take a notion to do it. I let you off too easy in that matter last summer, as it was, I'm thinking."

"You believed me guilty even though I denied it and would have railroaded me to the penitentiary if I had made a fight on the matter, so I let you have your way."

"Yes, and a good thing you did," came in a sneer from Main's lips. "For you were guilty all right. But I knew you would be of more use to me outside of jail than in, with a sword hanging over your head. I found my use for you when I sent you to get the cashier's job at Stokes."

"I've been careful, sir, not to mention to any one that you sent me or that I was ever in your employment. The members of the ship concern are not aware of it."

"You would have got your neck broken if you had told them," Main remarked. "Now, what about this young fellow who has come here to take charge?"

"He knows nothing about ship-building and he's not particularly efficient, I'd say."

For a moment "Gas" Main sat in thought. Then he looked up suddenly at the man standing before him.

"Did you have that other Stokes laid out with a plank?" he demanded, in a hostile voice.

"No, that was a pure accident."

"Well, don't let me hear of you trying to kill anybody, or injuring the ships," said he. "You're to find means to impede work and delay construction, but without violence. This is a financial scrap, not destruction and ruthlessness, bear in mind. That property is to be just as valuable when I'm done as when I begun, more so counting the ships building."

A sardonic smile flickered across the cashier's ascetic face, but was not seen by the gas company president.

"I'll be governed by your wishes," Mocket said.

"Have you heard anything about the Stokes and Johnson and Farrington?"

"No, Mr. Main."

"Do you think those bankers are worrying about the paper they hold?"

"It is possible. They made an appointment with

Mr. Robert Stokes for this morning. I should judge that they were growing somewhat anxious."

"Well, that will do now. I will look into that. Here is the two hundred you ask for," and Main went to his private safe.

"Thank you, sir," Mocket responded, as he received the bills. "I can assure you that it will be well spent."

"It had best be; I'm not throwing money away," Main growled; and without troubling to dismiss his tool he turned to his desk.

Mocket left the room. In the hallway outside the gas company's offices he turned his head for one bitter implacable glance at the door through which he had just come. When out of the building he passed along the street until he found an obscure hotel, where entering he ascended to a certain room. At a knock he was admitted by a strongly-built, middle-aged man, with blue eyes and a clipped, pointed, yellow beard.

"Ah, it is you," the man stated, with no especial cordiality.

"Yes. And my time is limited, for I must not be absent from the shipyard office so long as to start inquiries."

The bearded man stroked his beard, placed to his lips and lighted a china pipe.

"Briefness is wise, and we must not be seen too frequently together, even by the hotel people. I desire no attention attracted to myself."

"I thank you for meeting me at all," Mocket

stated. "Have you any information concerning my proposal?"

The eagerness in the question, as well as an excitement of manner restrained with difficulty, was apparent.

"Yes, this much," his companion stated. "That you will be permitted to make the trial. The materials will be furnished you; I and another will remain here to advise you. But it is to be understood that the undertaking is yours, the responsibility yours, and if need be the danger yours."

"I ask no more," Mocket exclaimed, vehemently.

"If you fail—well, it's at your own risk. If you succeed, I am authorized by a very high person whom I shall not name to say that it will go far towards reinstating you in your former rights, in obliterating the past, in restoring your name. That very high person will make a recommendation to such a purpose with those in whom lies the power to forgive; and the recommendation undoubtedly will be received with favor."

Mocket suddenly covered his face with his hands; his body shook with emotion.

"I have been an exile so long!" he cried. "Once again I want to set my feet upon my native soil. I am ready to give my life to see my honor clean, to be able to hold up my head among my former friends, to use my real name—that name, as you know, that has a 'von.' I swear my disgrace was brought upon me by another, that I was his victim

and have carried my shame these five years because——"

"That is neither here nor there," the other coolly
interrupted. "The point is that now you have your
chance to regain what you lost. This is the opportunity; and the trial is to be yours alone. If you
perform a valuable service, such as you propose, it
will receive recognition; it will be a long step in
your rehabilitation. That is the message I carry in
answer."

Mocket straightened, looking at the speaker with
a fanatical fire burning in his black eyes.

"Nothing shall stop me—I shall carry it through!"

"That is good spirit. When you've finished I'm
authorized to take you with me for further service," the other said, in a more friendly tone.

"That is splendid! I shall prove myself to you
and those in authority, prove myself by a hundred
deeds. Let them send me to the dangerous places,
on the perilous errands. I burn to give myself utterly to my country, to show where lies my heart
and my soul! I will rise through fire if need be
to my former position of honor, when again I may
wield my officer's sword, trusted and esteemed! No
sacrifice shall be too great!"

"Good, very good."

"My life in this accursed land, in this accursed
spot, has been wretched and debasing," he went on.
"A hundred times I could have killed men whose
blood is the blood of coarse swine, but from whose
hands I have had to receive the money on which I

live. Money accompanied by insults! Insults to me
—one of a noble family! At home I would have
run them through! And now you hold out the hope
that it shall end; I give you thanks from the very
depths of my heart!"

As if long frozen springs had been thawed,
Mocket poured forth this utterance in a torrent. On
his working face was written the bitter ignominy he
had suffered and the resentment he felt. He held a
hand aloft as if to invoke on every one and everything alien about him the hatred of his impassioned
soul.

Then at last he ceased to speak, remained for a
little standing motionless, silent, looking beyond the
bearded man.

"Well, possibly you will excuse this outburst," he
remarked finally, in his natural tone.

"It is understandable," the other replied.

"You'll hear no more of it. Now when shall I
meet with you again to discuss my plan?"

"When you leave the shipyard for the day. The
quicker matters are arranged, the better. Once we
have agreed upon your course, it will be seldom necessary to confer, except on vitally important details."

Mocket wiped and replaced his eye-glasses upon
his nose.

"I'll come here straight from the shipyard this
evening," said he. "And now, good day."

XI

ELLEN DURAND

TEN days had passed since Robert Stokes arrived and took hold of the shipyard. But so far as Ellen Durand could see no progress had been made towards uncovering the conspiracy being carried on against the company. And this in spite of the fact that an attempt had been feebly carried out to wreck a switch engine and string of cars in the yard. Some one had driven an iron wedge into a frog, but fortunately the cars were moving slowly when the first wheel struck the obstruction, so that beyond one truck leaving the rails and the cars and engine receiving a severe jolt no harm was done. Stokes did not even mention the occurrence in the office; she learned of it casually in the front room.

His first appearance had aroused in her a lively curiosity as to his competence to meet the situation; he himself had seemed confident enough. But his confidence had not materialized into action. He had taken up the routine work of the office; he gave a good deal of attention to the shipyard; he busied himself with details;—that was all. Since the first afternoon he had never discussed with her the subject of the attacks on the business. He had not even dictated a letter to the Seattle office concerning the matter. The hope that he might bring the criminals to justice, which he had inspired, gradually yielded to disappointment. For the life of her, she could not see how any man whose business was imperiled could continue so unperturbed and passive!

She herself experienced a constant if vague uneasiness. Not for herself, to be sure, but for the company, for the ships, and, indeed, for him. It was as if the air of the place was charged with subtle danger, which at some unexpected moment should collect and strike. She could feel it in the very atmosphere of the office. She breathed it every time she stepped forth from the building. The great shapes of the vessels that were building, despite the clatter of hammers, were heavy with it. She could not shake off the undefined dread.

"Miss Durand, either the work is beginning to tell on you or you've something dreadful on your conscience, for you're looking fagged," Bob remarked one afternoon, after a scrutiny of her face.

"I know it's not the work, if I do look that way —and there's nothing on my conscience that I'm aware of," she smiled.

"Well, you're a little pale anyway. We can't afford to have you breaking down or anything like that. It's bad enough the company has to put up with a new manager just at this time; a new and inexperienced stenographer would probably send it on the rocks. So with your permission I'm going to prescribe fresh air. I've the use of a motor boat belonging to a neighbor of my brother's, and I'd be pleased to give you a run after dinner this evening. An hour or two on the water will fill you so full of ozone that you'll want to start for Washington at once and wave a suffragette's banner in the President's face."

The twitch at the corner of her mouth grew, until at last she broke into a laugh. Then she gave a nod.

"I'll be glad to go on the water," said she. "The picture you draw of me as I'd conduct myself in front of the White House makes me ambitious. It might lead in time to my being arrested, like Mrs. Pankhurst, and being thrust into jail, which would make me famous."

"I'll call for you a little after seven o'clock tonight—we should make an early start. Tell me where to come, please."

She named the street number of the house where she boarded, then added doubtfully:

"I suppose nothing serious will happen here while you're out of telephone reach."

"Can't help it if it does." He fixed his gaze on her face. "I believe that's what's worrying you. Afraid something will occur to the plant. Is that it?"

"Well, naturally since Mr. Frederic Stokes was hurt I've been anxious, somewhat. I've wondered what the next accident would be."

Stokes shoved his hands into his pocket and grinned at her.

"Observe yours truly," said he. "You don't see

lines of worry furrowing my visage, do you? Nix, not, no. Worry never got a person anything but insomnia and a ticket of admission to an insane asylum. Do everything possible to prevent trouble, but never lie awake to see whether you can invent troubles that don't exist, or to fret about what you don't know. Ruins one's appetite. That doesn't mean one shouldn't saw wood when he's working— he should. But worry isn't work; it's waste. There, I've delivered my first and last sermon in Martinsport. Expect me to come bounding up the steps of your domicile at seven-fifteen with a motor boat under one arm and a couple of villains under the other to ease your mind."

"That would help wonderfully," she exclaimed, her eyes glowing.

But one may conjecture that the villains had little to do with the glow. At the prospect of an evening excursion upon the water the fear that had haunted her was forgotten too; it was replaced by the flutter of anticipation every girl has before a treat.

Circumstances had contrived to restrict Ellen Durand's life in Martinsport to a dead level,—circumstances and possibly temperament. Thrown on her own resources after the long illness and death of her widowed mother, she had turned to the only work that would immediately afford an income. She had just finished her second year in a small college when her mother fell ill, and being warned by the doctor that her mother's death was inevitable, while realizing that their moderate means would also be exhausted by consequent expenses, she had studied stenography in preparation for the future. After the first pain of her mother's death had passed, she had come from her home in the central part of the state to Martinsport, as the latter had been recommended as a growing city, small but offering opportunities. It chanced that she arrived about the time Stokes Brothers opened its office. At her boarding-house she met Andrews, who on learning she sought a place as a stenographer had suggested her to Frederic Stokes as probably a satisfactory employee; Andrews having just been hired by the firm and knowing that a stenographer was desired.

This is the bare outline of her advent in Martinsport. It does not include the homesickness, the doubts, the fears with which she ventured forth to the strange town and began her work of earning a livelihood. It does not reckon the hard necessity of foregoing her college aspirations in order to attend to the dispiriting task of wage-earning. It does not recite the feelings of loneliness and loss in being compelled to surrender the pleasures, the gayeties and the friends that she one time had. This part of her experience was buried in her soul.

Aside from an occasional evening with Andrews at a moving picture show, her regular church attendance on Sundays, strolls with some of the girls at her boarding-house, she lived almost as solitarily as if in the midst of a desert. The rather noisy and flippant men friends of her companions, to whom she was introduced, neither interested nor attracted her. And reserved by nature as she was, without superficial prettiness, content to keep her fineness of character rather than sacrifice it to gain popularity with those men, she was considered slow. The shallowness of their minds and purposes bored her, while on their part they were constrained by a feeling that she was different if not superior, though she never talked of herself or revealed her thoughts or affairs. Possibly that was the reason she perplexed them: she did not on first acquaintance chatter of everything she knew, or had done, or had seen; she did not even speak the glib, slangy phrases that largely constituted language with their kind. Altogether, they could not make her out; she was a bit of a mystery. And so she was let alone.

She employed her leisure time mostly in reading. She still had her dreams. That she should not always remain a stenographer she was resolved, though when she should escape and what she should be and do she had not yet planned. The determination, for determination it was and not mere hope, buoyed her spirit so that she was able to pursue her work steadfastly and preserve a cheerful demeanor.

Thus it was when Robert Stokes invited her to ride upon the water that evening, after months of an existence bereft of even little pleasures, she felt an anticipatory delight all out of proportion to the event. Until the moment she had not realized how starved for social recreation she was. The unexpectedness of the excursion gave it a happier charm, moreover, while the prospect of being with a man of the kind she had been previously accustomed to know, as his guest, set her pulses to beating. Her spirits seemed to feel a sudden release.

In a state of vivacity she found it difficult to conceal she hurried to her room at the end of the day to press her prettiest silk waist anew and to arrange her hair. Never did one have such turbulent, unruly black hair; it simply wouldn't behave! Her struggle with it put a delicate pink in her cheeks. At the supper table her eyes shone beneath their long dusky lashes with a bright luminosity that caused a young fellow across from her, a clerk, to stare.

"Take a look at that Durand girl," he whispered to a companion. "Some class, eh? Didn't know she was so good-looking."

"Well, it ain't exactly good looks; it's more—well, as you say, class. Like the movie vampires have," was the other's reply, after a critical inspection of Ellen Durand.

"I get you," said the first, "maybe we've been overlooking the lady. I think I'll get better acquainted with her. Might take her to the Princess show—good picture there to-night, 'A Faithful Magdalene,' with cabaret scenes and all that."

But when after supper he pursued his purpose of becoming better acquainted with Ellen Durand, inviting her to attend the "show," she thanked him and politely pleaded another engagement. And shortly afterward Robert Stokes, garbed in cool gray and wearing a straw hat of fine texture, appeared and bore her off under a battery of boarders' eyes.

"Gee, who's that gentleman!" one of a group of girls exclaimed, resuming her gum-chewing. "Strolled up and took her away and never batted an eye."

"That Bangkok hat cost not less than twenty dollars," said one of the clerks, with the authoritative air of a person who knew whereof he spoke. He clerked in a gentlemen's furnishings shop.

"Well, she might have introduced us," said another girl, patting her hair.

"I wonder what he sees in her," said a third. "She isn't a bit clever or stylish."

And the talk drifted off into a discussion of Ellen Durand's shortcomings.

XII

THE ADVENTURE AT THE ISLAND

THE sea lay smooth, undisturbed by even the
lightest breeze, undulating gently to the swell that
came in lazily from the gulf. On the western hori-
zon the sun had just sunk from sight, leaving a
pink glow in the sky whose reflection stained the
waters. The shore with its piers and ships at
anchor, its mass of business buildings, its long row
of white mansions to the west, lying against a
dark green background of trees and wood growth,
extended in a panorama that seemed to expand before Ellen Durand's and Bob Stokes' eyes as their
boat moved at half speed on its way. About them
were the small craft of other pleasure-seekers—
cat-boats, launches, dories, canoes, passing hither
and thither. Far out in the channel, whose beacons
were already burning against the coming night, a
steamer trailed a line of smoke low on the water.

With half closed eyes, breathing the balmy air
with languorous delight, a smile on her lips, Ellen
Durand for a time observed the scene with no desire for talk. Martinsport appeared far off, unreal,
as if in truth it were floating away. The motion of

137

the boat lulled her. The expanse of sea and sky soothed her mind.

But presently she came back to life.

"You'll wonder whether I've lost my tongue, Mr. Stokes, if I remain still any longer," she said, "but this is my first time on the water here, or anywhere, for an age. I've been drinking the beauty of it in, reveling in it, so that I shall remember the pleasure it gives me. I didn't wish to miss a single bit!"

"I knew you were enjoying it—and so was I," he answered. Then he added, "And I'm glad you didn't spoil it with a lot of worn-out adjectives. I'm always filled with foreboding when a person immediately burst out with 'Gorgeous!'—'Grand!'— 'Glorious!' — 'Marvelous!' — before he or she has——"

"It's usually a 'she,'" she interrupted, with a nod.

"Well, before she has taken more than a look, for that will be the end of it with her and next breath she'll be rattling away about something somebody said about nothing in particular. Her appreciation stops with that one fizz—'Grand—gorgeous!'"

She began to laugh.

"I know people your description exactly fits," she remarked. "They fizz in just that way for an instant like bottles of pop, and are then exhausted. I feel almost sorry for them."

"'More to be pitied than censured,'" Bob quoted.

"But I fear it would be sympathy wasted, at that. Now, to go back, you said this was your first time on the water—we'll try and make up for it. One needs diversion, and boating so far as I've seen is the best Martinsport has."

The shadowed, enigmatical look he had perceived before came into her eyes. She gazed for a little while out upon the sea.

"What appeals to me about a big city, like New York, is not only the diversions but the whole life of it, the opportunities, the spirit, the energy, the mystery. I've never been there, or, indeed, to any great city. But I've read of them. Martinsport's no more than a town. Of course, one expects to work, or at any rate be occupied, wherever one is, but to feel one's self a part of flowing streets and the hidden tremendous force that makes up a big city must certainly be a satisfaction. It's the gathering place of wealth, brains, power. Everything is there for one to see, know, feel, enjoy."

"One's work in a city becomes routine, as anywhere else," Bob stated.

"Yes; that is taken for granted. But there remains the part of a person that work doesn't touch. Why, I could feast my eyes on things in the windows there, that I'd never see anywhere but there, though I might never expect to own them. One too would be rubbing elbows with people of every nation and race, whose occupations and habits and thoughts and ambitions could only be guessed at. And there are the galleries, the concerts, the the-

aters, and all that. It's not just any single thing
in a big city; it's everything combined that makes
life in it an adventure. Yes, no other word will do
—and it seems to me life ought to be an adventure.
Every day of it!"

As she spoke, the glow had deepened in her eyes
until they were radiant. But almost immediately
this died and her brows drew together brooding.

"Adventures may be dangerous, especially in a
large city," Stokes stated.

"Better danger than a life of deadly dullness,"
she answered. "But one can usually avoid danger
if one will."

"I almost believe you've made up your mind to
go to a big city."

"Yes, next autumn," she replied, staring at the
water. "I couldn't endure Martinsport longer than
that. I shall go then. It's not dissatisfaction with
my work, understand. Mr. Frederic Stokes has
been most kind. But it's the rest of it." And she
indicated the town by a wave of her hand.

"If you think it quiet here, you ought to spend
a few months in the woods to get the idea out of
your head," Stokes said, smiling.

• Possessing as he himself did an active spirit, he
sympathized with her in her desire to escape from
a situation that must be both dull and distasteful.
Daily contact with her in the office had led him to
recognize her intelligence and good breeding. At
her boarding-house he had seen the showy and rather vulgar girls and young fellows—their dress and

airs bespoke their kind!—with whom she was forced to associate. To one of Ellen Durand's fine sensibilities the day-in-and-day-out commingling with them would not only serve to depress her mind but would arouse all the rebellious feelings in her nature.

As she did not respond to his last words, he studied her in silence. She could be more than rebellious, he decided, she was capable of stormy passion, given the incentive. He perceived that her calmness was restraint and that he knew not what fires smoldered within her soul. And with these impressions he felt a new and growing interest in the girl.

All the while the motor boat glided leisurely westward along the shore. The piers were left behind. The white homes, surrounded by trees and fronting the beach, moved past in a procession. The quick night of the south was descending upon land and water, promising presently to blot out the scene. It was just then that a powerfully engined launch overtook and passed them, its exhaust exploding noisily. As the boat moved by scarcely a hundred feet away, the lone man in the craft shed his coat and tossed it aside. The air puffed it like a sail, blew something resembling a colored handkerchief from an inner pocket and then let the coat subside in the bottom of the launch. The owner had not observed what occurred. The boat went steadily ahead. On the surface of the water floated the colored square of cloth.

Stokes gave his own boat a sheer in the direction of the article.

"That had the look of a flag to me," he explained. "And not an American flag, either. I had a glimpse of three broad stripes as it fluttered down. French, probably, from the design. There is quite a bit of French blood in this region."

As the boat came alongside of the thing, he scooped it up. He gazed at the dripping cloth, then an exclamation broke from his lips.

"That's not French," he said.

"What is it?"

"Take it by two corners and spread it open. Don't wet yourself. Now, see!"

It was a small silk flag, little larger than her two hands, in three broad bands of color—red, white and black. In the gentle breeze made by the movement of the boat it waved and whipped in the hold of her fingers.

"I never saw one like it before—or, yes, I have, now that I remember," she said, "but I can't place it."

"That's a German flag," Bob stated.

"Why, we're fighting Germany! What should any one be doing with its flag?"

"The government will ask the same thing if it gets hold of him. Wait a moment now! I want to keep track of that fellow!"

Increasing speed, he set the motor boat in chase of the other, now some quarter of a mile ahead. The twilight died out rapidly, darkness fell. Along

the beach the arc lights flashed forth like a row of gems, while overhead the stars began to appear. The shape of the unknown's launch was still visible against the faint illumination of the western sky and the sheen of water.

"Won't he see us?" Ellen Durand questioned, with repressed excitement.

"I think not. We've the advantage in respect to lights. And he'll not hear us, because his own exhaust is pretty loud. This little kicker of ours is keeping even with him, thank goodness! If he doesn't go too far or speed up we'll learn something of this gentleman who carries an enemy flag."

Gradually the leading boat bent away from the shore.

"I can't see his craft any more," the girl said.

"We're following. I believe he's making for that little island we perceived just before it grew dark. It lies two or three miles off the land and can't be very far now. We ought to be able to see the loom of it presently."

"Well, don't bump into it, please."

"You shouldn't mind. Awhile ago you were longing for an adventure; now you have it. Not every person has wishes fulfilled so quickly."

But it is doubtful if she heard.

"I see the island!" she cried.

"Whisper, please," he cautioned. "We may not be welcome and there may even be for us a little danger. I'm going to shut off the exhaust and

proceed slowly, in order to give him time to land. If we can steal in without any sound, we'll do so. I wonder what the fellow's up to out here at night!"

"I don't hear anything."

"He's landed. We'll try farther along the beach. Now, we must be quiet. Voices carry on the water and we'll be heard."

Making the beach at a spot some distance from where the other man must have touched, Bob Stokes helped his companion to disembark, drew the little craft up on the sand as far as he could and hooked its anchor in a log against which he stumbled. In the starlight the beach and tree growth of the island were dimly visible. Across the water eastward the lights of Martinsport gleamed far away.

"You wait here while I reconnoiter," he said to Ellen Durand. "I'll not be gone long."

She caught his sleeve.

"No, sir, I'll go, too. If I stayed here alone, I'd be frightened for fear something happened to you. What if you didn't come back! And I'm just as eager to find out things as you are."

"But——" Bob began.

Her grasp tightened.

"I'm not afraid with you, but I'd see men on every side of me if I were left alone here in the dark. Why, we're miles from home! I'm going to keep my hold on you, Mr. Stokes, and go wherever you go. Don't you try to make me stay; I'm absolutely going with you."

"But it will be really much safer here," he protested.

"No. And I'll not be a bit of trouble to you. Come on, I'm not even going to listen." She gave a little pull on his sleeve.

"Well, I came here to find out something, so I guess there's nothing else for it," he stated. "Don't shriek, whatever happens. Just drop down and play dead."

"I shall. But don't leave me."

Slipping his arm into hers, he led her along the beach, searching the darkness before them and pausing from time to time to hearken. Only the low sound of the water lapping the sand came to their ears. They could distinguish each other's figures, but little else. A dim silken shimmer moved on the surface of the sea.

"There's something!" Ellen Durand breathed, after a time.

A line blacker than the darkness extended into the water. Bob stared at it.

"A small pier," he whispered. "His boat's likely anchored at the end of it. Let me take your hand and lead; we'll turn in here."

The beach sloped gently upward for twenty or thirty feet, where the trees began. Taking his bearings from the pier, he drew the girl along until they stood in the gloom of the woods, apparently in a path cleared through the undergrowth. They advanced slowly, their feet making no sound on the sand, and with the scent of pines all about them. Her fingers shut faster on his.

All at once he halted. A beam of light shone through the trees before them.

"I think our man's there," he murmured.

"Aren't we going nearer?"

"Certainly—come along."

He led her forward again, keeping a hand before him for obstacles and exercising every care to be silent. As he approached he saw the light came from a window and toward this he directed his steps, by alternate moves and pauses, until he made out the side of the house. Apparently it was a dwelling of no large size. At one end he beheld a glow where the light fell through an open door.

A figure passed before the window, then appeared in the doorway. It was that of a short, stout man, who smoked a pipe and fanned himself with a palm-leaf fan. Situated as the small house was in the midst of the trees, it was shut away from any cooling draught from the water. He fanned himself and wiped his neck with a handkerchief and looked out into the darkness, with slow regular puffs at his pipe.

"It is warm, very warm—ach, I would give much to bury my face in a cold stein!" A voice within murmured a reply, at which the smoker in the doorway continued, "Yes, the time is short. And when we are come where there is beer, I'll take me a bath in it." He turned about and moved out of sight again.

Stokes drawing Ellen Durand along with him circled the end of the house, until he found cover behind a clump of bushes ten paces or so before the door. Crouching there and parting the leaves they beheld a section of a room directly in line of vision. It was evident from the dilapidated state of the interior that the house had been long abandoned and given over to decay, which made its present tenancy all the more strange. No effort had been put forth to improve the place, indeed, all the signs made clear that its occupancy was but temporary—suitcases lying open but not unpacked on the floor, the pair of folding cots, the table knocked together out of boards, a small oil-stove for cooking, the lantern hanging by a cord from a rafter and the cheap glass lamp on the table, a row of large mineral water bottles against a wall, several wooden boxes in the middle of the floor with lids ripped partly off. Everything indicated brief possession. The stuff in the room had no value; the men could depart on a minute's notice.

Two men were at the table:—one sitting, a fair man with a pointed yellow beard, his cap pushed back on his head; the other, the smoker who had appeared in the door, standing across from and looking down at him. The former had a number of objects on the board where his hands rested, which he examined, now lifting one to inspect it, now another, and again fitting them together as if they were parts of a whole. From time to time the second man would remove his pipe, explain something, point a finger at this and at that, give a wave of his hand, stroke his mustache reflectively, speak anew or nod.

"The man sitting was the fellow in the boat," Stokes whispered to his companion. "I wish I could hear what they're saying."

"That thing he's manipulating, what is it?" she queried, low.

"I can't make it out."

Again the smoker was pointing at the various objects on the table. Finally he laid down his pipe and walked to one of the suitcases, whence he brought a folded sheet of paper. This he spread open before his friend. The latter alternately studied it and the parts of the mechanism before him.

"We'll go back to the window," Bob told the girl. "Perhaps we can get under it and learn what they're at. I've a suspicion these men are up to something that ought to be known and guarded against."

She caught his arm and pressed it.

"You must be careful though," she returned, anxiously.

"I'll be prudence itself—I have you with me."

"It's not of myself I'm thinking, but of you," said she. "You have the responsibility of the company now, so you mustn't take any unnecessary risks. I don't want you to take the notion into your head, presently, to walk in and interview these men."

Stokes laughed under his breath. He could not

see Ellen Durand in the darkness, but he was aware she was gazing at him.

"Never fear," said he.

"Well, then, I'm ready to creep with you to the window," she whispered.

Retracing their way to the point where they had turned aside, they stealthily advanced to the side of the house. From the window sash the glass panes had long since disappeared and over the openings mosquito netting had been tacked. When Bob's outstretched fingers touched the weather boarding of the structure he stopped, gave Ellen Durand a warning touch on the shoulder, tucked her arm in his to assure her and stood motionless, hearkening. The pair had a position just without the edge of the panel of light falling from the window. Assailing their nostrils was the musty smell that clings to damp, decaying habitations.

Stokes felt a little quiver of Ellen Durand's body, as if the solitude and dismal character of the old dwelling had caused her to recoil. He was about to press her arm to give her courage, when he heard the men inside the room get to their feet. Then he saw the short, stout man remove the lantern from the cord and blow out the light on the table.

"I'll take you there," the fellow said.

The mysterious strangers went toward the door.

XIII

WHAT OCCURRED AT THE OLD WRECK

STOKES quickly led his companion away from the spot, feeling his road before him in the gloom. Encountering a heavy vine that overspread a tree trunk, he drew her behind this, indeed scarcely gaining the shelter when the lantern appeared about the corner of the house.

The two men came towards their concealment, reached it and brushed by while Bob and Ellen Durand breathlessly waited for them to pass. Pass they did, walking in silence and moving south in a direction that would take them across the narrow island, weaving in and out among the trees and bushes until the lantern as it grew more distant looked like a will-o'-the-wisp.

"We might as well follow and learn whatever's to be learned," Bob Stokes remarked. "Shall we?"

"I'm game," she replied, with a determined air which delighted the young fellow.

"You've more courage than some men," said he, as they started after the light.

"Or more curiosity, which is it?"

"I insist on it's being courage. Now give me your hand. You had best keep an arm up to shield

your face from twigs." And holding her fingers
in his he led the way forward.

The distance they had to go was not great, however, for the island was not more than four hundred yards across at its widest. A few minutes
of pursuing the lantern, whose faint gleams aided
them somewhat in avoiding trees, and they heard
the water along the southern beach.

They quickened their pace and reached the fringe
of the timber by the time the men had crossed the
stretch of sand to the water's edge. There a long,
low mass loomed black in the starlight, the hull of
a wrecked vessel, they perceived, when it came within the lantern's circle of radiance.

The men moved along the length of it. Apparently it was the bulk of some schooner cast on
the beach in a hurricane. The stern lay low and
half-buried in sand; the masts were gone. But the
upthrust bow and middle section rode high. Hoist-
ing themselves up on the stern the two men they
watched moved forward toward the waist of the
wrecked vessel, where, after a pause, they vanished,
light and all, as if by a trick of legerdemain.

"Gone down into the cabin," Stokes said.

"But what would they be doing there?"

"I'd give a good deal to know. I'm wondering
if we dare chance a nearer view."

"It's quite dark," Ellen Durand suggested.

"And we could hide under the hull. Anyway,
suppose they saw us. We should maintain that

we've as good a right as any one to be on this island."

"You'll not have to wait for me for fear of our discovery," she replied.

Before he had time to speak again, she sped forward towards the black shadow of the wreck, her shape vanishing. Stokes ran hurriedly after her, overtook her and together they came to a halt on the sand before the prow, where they listened for any sound that might come from the invisible men. All was silent about the wreck. They heard only the soft lapping of the sea as it washed against the beach.

"Come, we'll have a look at the other end," Bob said, catching up her hand again to keep her close by his side. "But we'll stay under the sea side of the hull where our chances are better of being unseen if those men should appear unexpectedly; they will descend to the beach where they mounted, on the other side."

Towards the stern they groped their way. Thrown up on the sand as the schooner had been by some huge wave, it lay in an oblique position with the quarter-deck nearest the water; indeed, they discovered the sand about the stern to be damp, and had their feet wet by the advancing slither of a wave.

"This will ruin your shoes," Bob breathed.

"No matter. What's a pair of slippers in an adventure!" was her low whisper.

As they arrived at the stern Stokes struck his shins against an obstruction, which on touching with his hand he found to be a small boat. Risking possible detection he lighted a match and held it in his cupped palms over the little craft; a row-boat drawn close up under the wreck, with oars stowed inboard, with fishing-lines lying on the seat, a number of fish shining dully on the bottom and a coat and disreputable old hat flung down in the bow.

Stokes extinguished the match, then for an instant took thought. Where was the fisherman? Was he somewhere along the beach, or was he in the abandoned wreck with the two men? If the latter, his fishing had been a pretense and he had come to meet the pair in a secret conference. Moreover, the fellow made one more enemy to look out for. Decidedly this island had a growing interest of its own.

Squeezing between boat and schooner Stokes and Ellen Durand reached a place where their heads were above the stern bulwark, which allowed them a view forward along the deck. The vessel very likely had been an oyster boat and was some sixty or seventy feet long, with a small trunk cabin in the waist from which the windows and door were missing, as Stokes observed against the lighted interior. The gleams of the lantern shone up the companion way not more than thirty feet from where he and the girl stood; the lantern itself he beheld through the opening suspended from a hook in the cabin roof; and above the deck level which pitched upward towards the bow he perceived in the cabin the heads and busts of three men, as if they were cut off below the armpits—the two men who had come with the lantern, and another, whom for a moment he could not clearly distinguish in the uncertain light.

Apparently all three were standing talking, now with a remark from one and now with a question or answer from another. The two men from the old house were giving earnest attention to the third man, about whom to Stokes there was a haunting familiarity of head and posture. The talk ran on in low, quick exchanges, sometimes reaching the hearers in a faint murmur, but for the most part, owing to the nearer sound of the waves, a mere pantomime. And then all at once the third man leaned forward speaking assertively, so that his bare head with its rumpled hair and his face came full and plain within the light.

A gasp escaped Ellen Durand. Stokes himself gave a start of surprise.

"Do you see who he is?" he whispered, in amazement.

"Yes; I recognize him. I remember now that he was absent from supper at the boarding-house," she went on, in his ear. "What in the world can he be doing here?"

"Doing his worst probably—and I should like to know just what that is. I've a strong suspicion this meeting has something which bears on our ship-yard matters."

"Mr. Andrews, of all persons!"

"Though I've suspected him of several things,

I'll confess I was surprised when he turned his face and I knew him," was Stokes' answer. "And he's here to meet men one of whom carried a little German flag!"

"But I can't believe he would be a traitor to —well, to America," she exclaimed in a horrified undertone.

"A fellow who is disloyal to his employers wouldn't find it a great step to be disloyal to his country."

A movement within the cabin indicated that the talk was at an end. A few more words were uttered, Andrews made an energetic gesture with his arm as if to end whatever was under discussion, as if in fact brushing the others' opinions aside, and taking a step to the cabin door vaulted up the companion way. He was half along the deck to where the observing pair stood when the men ascended after him, carrying the lantern, at which moment Bob Stokes drew his companion round the stern into the sheltering darkness.

Andrews leaped down upon the beach, pushed his boat upon the water, waded a little way out with it. There he paused to regard the men on deck, who had posted themselves at the side with lantern upheld in order to witness his departure. Holding the boat and standing knee-deep in the sea he looked up at them in silence, the light dimly showing his figure clothed in old trousers and shirt, his face grim and set.

None of the three spoke,—curious, that silence

too, Stokes thought. They remained thus for possibly a minute, after which Andrews climbed into his boat and seized the oars.

"Good evening, gentlemen," he shouted, and waved a hand. Then he set himself to rowing, pulling with long, powerful strokes, and disappeared upon the water.

The two on deck continued to watch after him for a time.

"Now he's gone, we must begin our work," said one, whom Bob imagined was the short, fleshy man. "You take the lantern and I'll get up that case of dynamite and we'll be off."

Their feet retreated. Venturing a glance along the deck, Stokes saw them once more descend into the cabin, whence after a moment's delay they reappeared. The man who had spoken carried a small box clasped against his stomach.

"Let us be going first," Bob whispered. "I shouldn't want them to happen on our boat if they should take it into their heads to prowl along the other beach."

"I'm ready." Ellen Durand stepped back as she spoke, then suddenly clutched her companion's arm struggling, while a sharp cry escaped her lips. "Help me, I've one foot in a hole!" she gasped.

Stokes quickly drew her up to his side out of the small unseen cavity washed under the hulk's sternpost.

"What happened?" he asked, low.

"Slipped into water up to my knee. I didn't mean to cry out."

He shot a look over the deck towards the two men. That they had heard Ellen Durand's voice and taken alarm was only too evident: the one had set his box on the planks at his feet, the other had raised the lantern, and both were hearkening fixedly with faces towards the spot. Next instant the bearded man exclaimed:

"Did you hear? Some one's spying!"

"At the stern, wasn't it? Listen again."

Stokes stood taut of body, scarcely breathing, his hands still gripping Ellen Durand's arms, every sense alert. In the succeeding quiet the soft and persistent swishing of the sea upon the beach was the only disturbing sound. In the darkness of the wreck and the night the upheld lantern was the only spot of light.

"I heard something clearly," the first man stated.

"Perhaps it was only the squeak of a rat or the squeal of a floating seagull," the other returned.

"No, that was a voice, a human voice."

"Then we had better investigate." After a pause, the short, fat man went on. "He couldn't have come back; he wouldn't have had time. And any way he would not cry out."

"Nein, no. It is some one else. Have you a pistol?"

"Here it is."

"Ah, good!" the bearded man exclaimed. "Come, we shall look."

Stokes noiselessly began to steal forward in the gloom of the hull, leading his companion. Both stooped below the line of the bulwark. On the deck they heard the men's feet pass, going toward the stern.

"Bring the light and we'll get down on the sand," came to their ears, with unpleasant distinctness.

As the two men came down the side of the ship to the beach, the escaping pair gained the cover of the upreared bow, from which dangerous spot Stokes immediately set off, leading Ellen Durand up the sloping stretch of sand to the wood. But before they reached this a brighter glow than the lantern's swept the sands; Bob glancing hastily over his shoulder saw that a strong electric torch had been brought into play, which apparently the bearded man of the motor boat had produced from a pocket. Moreover, he had moved in their direction while his companion remained to search about the hulk, and was systematically illuminating the beach all the way up to the nearby wood.

Diminished as was the electric lamp's light when it touched the trees, it sufficed to mark objects. It disclosed a line of storm-washed drift and seaweed. Darting over another space it revealed for an instant a half-buried log. It brought out the shadowy mass of timber. It served indeed to discover Stokes to the man just as the former pushed Ellen Durand before him into the wood and he himself entered.

A shout gave warning of the fact.

"Here to me, Hoffner, quick, with your pistol!" rang out on the beach.

Holding to Ellen Durand's arm, Stokes plunged ahead in the darkness, keeping an outstretched hand in front, which saved him more than once from colliding with a tree or from falling headlong into a bush. Low plants and creepers caught at his feet and at those of the girl. Once a pistol shot sounded and a bullet sped through the pine boughs above their heads.

"They don't see us; that was fired on a chance," he said assuringly to his companion. "They're not going to catch us, nor are they even going to see us."

Over his shoulder he could now behold the glow of the light among the trees. Slanting away from the shifting track of the beam, he nevertheless pressed forward towards the middle of the island, until at last he found it necessary to seek a hiding-place in a thicket of bushes. The pursuers had come uncomfortably near. Indeed, as they hastened past, the men were within fifty feet of the crouching youth and girl, while the light of the torch rested for a brief space on their very screen in its searching sweeps of the wood about.

"The man may be making for the house. We must prevent his entering there, at all hazards," the bearded searcher was saying as he went by. "After we look there we'll go over the whole island."

"Yes, we must find him."

As their voices dropped away, Stokes lifted the

girl to her feet once more and began to follow, taking advantage of the dancing glow to find a way among the trees. Shortly the dim shape of the old house appeared within the projected beam.

House, light and all were swallowed up in darkness when the men vanished inside the dwelling. Stokes circled towards where he knew the path to be, for he was determined to gain before his pursuers the north beach where lay his boat. At a window the torch flashed once or twice, then sounded the slam of a door, and again the glow of light darted into view. The men having searched the house were taking up the hunt anew without waste of time.

Once the beam of the electric torch swam over the wood, projecting illusive shadows from trees and bushes. One of the latter cast its shade over the fleeting pair, only to cease, whereupon Bob caught Ellen Durand in his arms, ran forward for a minute with the light threatening their discovery, and then came to a halt. He was now some sixty feet from the old dwelling, but at any moment the searchers might widen the scope of their circle. As the misty light again and again swept the place, he had a glimpse of a white streak on the earth nearby, the sandy path he sought. The illuminating glow darted forward and back and then returned once more to the immediate surroundings of the house.

Ellen Durand had remained unstirring in his arms during the pause. Her hand rested on his shoulder and a strand of her hair brushed his cheek.

He could feel the quick beating of her heart. When the light had first shot among the trees about them, a little gasp had escaped her lips, but that was all.

"We'll go on now," he whispered.

"If you'll set me down, I'll walk," she said.

"Wait until we're farther off. I've located the path and I remember its direction, even in the dark —I'm used to woods. Besides, you can watch what goes on behind us."

Advancing until he found the path under his feet, he set forward slowly but steadily. His companion from time to time observed the glow of the torch as it appeared and reappeared, reporting its movements.

"I think the men are on the opposite side of the house," she said, "or we're getting farther away. I've lost it altogether.

"We're leaving the place," said he, "and we'll be out of this in a moment. I think I hear the water."

All at once her fingers closed on his coat.

"I see it again, the light! Back among the trees!" she cried.

"Then they are coming here for a look. They won't catch us."

Even as he spoke, he emerged upon the beach and they felt the coolness from the water upon their faces. He placed her upon the sand and turned about to examine the wood. A glimmer shone from the direction they had come.

"No time to lose; we must run," he said.

Taking her hand, he started. They sped along the beach towards the spot where they had left their boat, running side by side, keeping close to the water where the sand was smooth and hard, until Bob said they must pull up. Moving therefore at a walk, they presently made out in the starlight the black form of their craft.

Bob sprang to the log and loosened the anchor.

"There they are; they've come out!" Ellen Durand said.

"I see," said he.

He stepped forward, put his strength against the boat and pushed it off the sand, then straightened up to watch. A hundred yards away a bright disk moved slowly on the beach, stopped, circled and stopped again.

"Very likely they see our foot-prints," said he. "We must get as far out on the water as possible before they come in this direction."

Assisting her to embark, he gave the boat a push and leaped in. By means of the anchor he worked its bow about, at the same time shoving the craft away from shore. He dared not start the engine, the sound of which would instantly betray their whereabouts, but must trust to the current to bear the boat along, which here as along the whole coast had an eastward set. At last he lifted the anchor in.

"We're moving now, thank heaven!" said he.

"And so are those men, see," Ellen Durand responded.

The light approached along the beach. Its round glow touched the water, which trembled and gleamed under the radiance. All at once the torch went out.

"They're going to hunt us now in the dark. Afraid they themselves may be seen, likely as not," Bob remarked. "Or they think if we haven't yet put off, they'll find our boat. So much the better for us."

Their words were guarded. The water would still carry a loud tone to the men walking on the sand. As nearly as Bob could determine, the current carried the boat along the island at a rate that kept the interval about even, but their little vessel still remained only twenty-five or thirty yards from shore. If the searchers discovered their quarry close at hand upon the water, they might either open fire with the pistol or return to the pier and make pursuit in the launch.

Ellen Durand at length leaned towards Stokes.

"Those wretches are enemies. Did you hear what they said of dynamite?" she asked in a whisper.

"Yes. And I intend to see that they are rounded up."

"What are they planning?"

"Some bomb outrage—that was a bomb they examined and discussed in the house, I know now.

They must be arrested before they do any damage."

A quick breath sounded from the girl.

"The ships! Your ships! I know it!"

"I'm going to act as soon as we reach town," Bob stated. "I shall notify the police, secure their aid, come back here and get these fellows. Can't afford to delay a minute, whether it's our ships or something else they aim to destroy."

"And what of Mr. Andrews?" she asked.

"If the police catch these men, I'll include him in the arrest and see if he can't be made to confess the whole plot; if the men get away, as they're likely to do now they're alarmed, why, I shall let Andrews keep on as clerk till he again leads us to his accomplices and employers."

"Strange as it may seem, I can't make myself believe he's guilty," she said, slowly. "I always thought him sincere and straightforward and honest."

"Your feelings do you credit, but I'm afraid in his case they are mistakenly bestowed in his favor. To-night's revelations show him up in a clear light."

"It seems so," she agreed, a little sorrowfully.

But if Andrews' guilt appeared certain to Stokes, the young fellow's various connections with the plot were more than obscure, as were those of other interested persons. Where did Johnson and Farrington figure in the scheme against the shipyard? Where Broussard? The former two would not lend themselves to any alien attack upon the Stokes

property; that notion might at once be dismissed.
But Broussard? Was he scoundrel enough to associate himself with a plan to destroy the yard, or
any American property in fact? And yet that the
man was covertly working against the firm Bob was
convinced.

He finally gave the mystery up for the present;
it was too deep.

"If these men here could but be seized!" he said,
voicing his thought.

"You yourself will come back with the police?"
she asked.

"By all means. They will need a guide, for one
thing; for another, I wouldn't skulk at home."

She appeared to meditate this.

"Well, please do me a favor," said she, finally.

"Yes."

"Just stand behind a tree, if those men start
shooting when you and the police go after them.
Let somebody else be shot—I may want another
boat-ride."

Stokes yielded to a low laugh. Then he reached
out and patted her hand.

"And you shall have many of them. Not one
girl in a thousand would have kept as cool to-night
as you've done. Consider me your gondolier hereafter—and we'll keep the boat busy!"

The sea bore them steadily onward. The island
was at last passed, and sank into the night. Once
again only, for a moment, they perceived the torch

flash forth, when they were well away from the place. Then the light vanished. Fifteen minutes later Stokes started the engine and the little motor boat sped for the twinkling lights of Martinsport.

"I'm beginning to like the south," said Bob, in connection with nothing that had been said.

Ellen Durand made no answer. At the instant she had been thinking of herself held close in his arms during their escape from the house, her heart feeling the beat of his. He had thought her cool; but her mind had been a tumult of confused feelings. The very recollection made her pulses throb faster. And at his words her cheeks for no accountable reason grew warm. She thanked her lucky stars it was dark so that he could not see her face.

XIV

UNDER SUSPICION

Bob Stokes had not accompanied Ellen Durand
to her boarding-house after their return to Martinsport, for both recognized the urgent necessity of
securing police aid without a moment's loss of time
in order if possible to apprehend and arrest the
conspirators who made the little island their hiding-
place. When Bob had escorted her to the main
business street to place her on a street car that
would carry her home, he said:

"In a way this has spoiled our evening——"

"No, no; it has made it worth while," she interrupted quickly. "I only wish I were a man, so
that I could go with you and share in the finish.
Don't imagine that a girl—a real, alive girl, I
mean—cares only for a placid, undisturbed existence, whose most exciting events are receiving can-
dy and flowers and going to dances. There are such
girls, yes—but, goodness gracious, what kind of
girls are they and what, if anything, have they in
their heads! But it's such happenings and such experiences as this of to-night that I want; things
that grip and thrill a person. Why, this evening's
adventure is worth a hundred years of ordinary

167

dead-level existence! Perhaps to-morrow I'd not say this, but I'm still excited with it all and the truth will bubble out."

She looked up at Bob with eager smiling face and shining eyes.

"Good! That's what I like—spirit," he said. "If you had shown that our chase through the woods had upset you, that you were annoyed because your foot was wet and you had been whacked by bushes, and that you preferred to recline languidly and comfortably on a seat in the boat than run a risk of mussing your dress, I should never have asked you to go boating again. No straw figures for me, thank you! See, I'm talking straight out, too. And if we don't have a thousand more rides on the water, more or less, it will be because the sea has dried up."

"But you mustn't expose yourself needlessly when you go back with the police for those men, Mr. Stokes, or we may not get to take those boat rides," she responded, with a note of uneasiness marking her tones. "Those men may be desperate, in fact, I'm sure they will be desperate, for didn't they fire at us with a pistol? They will be on the lookout now. They——"

"If they haven't fled; that's my one fear," Bob put in.

"Why don't you go on to police headquarters? I mustn't keep you longer, and there's not the least reason in the world for your waiting here with me. A car will come in a minute."

Stokes glanced along the street, hesitated, then shook his head.

"I'll stay until it does come," said he, decisively.

Hard on his words however the particular car for which they waited came in sight.

"Now, don't worry about what may happen to me, for nothing is going to happen," he said as he assisted her to mount the car platform, at the same time giving her an assuring clasp of hand.

"Be careful just the same," she replied, earnestly. "I shall be anxious. That island seems much more dangerous to me now than it did when we were there."

Next instant the street car was carrying her away from the spot and as she glanced back she caught but a glimpse of Bob Stokes' tall figure striding off. And her thoughts continued to follow the young fellow, thoughts that were apprehensive and not a bit doughty now since the prospective danger concerned him alone, while she sat staring out the car window at the dimly lighted avenue along which she was being borne.

With his leaving her she suffered a depression of spirits and as it were a lack of purpose, which in truth was but the natural reaction following the exciting events of the evening. It was as if she had been swept forward for a time into a different and more impetuous current of life, where strange unbelievable things occurred, where wild lawless minds strove and dark passions ruled, where one moved in the chill shadow of death, and then suddenly had been swirled forth again into quiet, accustomed waters. All that had happened by the old abandoned house and at the wreck on the beach and in the gloom of the wood now seemed like a fantastic dream. For, was not this street car jogging along as it always did? Were not the other passengers riding to their homes in the same tired, preoccupied manner as ever? Did Martinsport show any sign of activity more than it usually did at this time of night?

Arriving at her boarding-house she felt no desire for sleep. The porch was untenanted, the grouped chairs alone remaining where the other boarders had sat when earlier in the evening she took her departure with Robert Stokes under the fire of their inquisitive eyes. Doubtless the young fellows and girls had dispersed to the "movies" or on walks, or other amusements, and had not yet returned, as the hour was still early. So here she seated herself to become again absorbed in the recollection of her adventure and the confused emotions it aroused.

Vaguely she realized the events of the night for her signified a change. The gray curtain which hid the future had parted a little way; it appeared trembling as if about to be drawn wholly aside. To reveal what? To affect her how? To allow her to walk ahead to what joys or what pain? Feelings rather than thoughts made her aware that go forward she must to whatever might be. Perhaps Robert Stokes would be involved in that future, perhaps not, but in any event her eager nature would press on to a full experience of life.

It was possibly an hour later that a step on the walk awoke her from her introspection. By the light of a street lamp that fell on the front of the house she recognized the advancing youth as Andrews. He wore the old hat and rough clothes in which he had been garbed when she beheld him on the deck of the old hulk talking to the two strangers. Until now she had forgotten him altogether, but she at once grasped the fact that his return in a rowboat from the island must necessarily have been slow. Indeed, he could not have been much past the point of the island when Stokes and she were speeding from it in the motor boat.

He perceived her sitting in the shadow as he mounted the porch steps, peered at her when he came nearer and finally made her out.

"Oh, it's you, Miss Durand," said he, in a relieved tone. "I'll sit down, too, for a few minutes if I don't intrude; I'm tired. Was afraid you might be one of the peroxide crowd, who give me the jim-jams."

Ellen Durand had straightened in her chair, alert, curious, and amazed that she did not immediately experience a feeling of repulsion for the young man. He did not look in the least like a conspirator; he appeared quite natural and ordinary.

"What have you been doing, fishing?" she inquired, without too great a display of interest.

"Yes. But I didn't have much luck. Caught one or two white trout, but mostly croakers and cat which are no good. Didn't get enough fish to make it worth bringing them home."

"Well, you might take your friends along some time when you go out on the water. Don't you think a girl ever likes to boat ride?"

"I'll ask you next time," said Andrews. "But we won't fish then, unless you put on old clothes. Fish mess things up."

"Where did you go?"

"Oh, one can fish anywhere outside the harbor." Andrew gave an indefinite wave of his hand.

"You don't seem to be very enthusiastic about it," Ellen Durand stated. "Perhaps you haven't gone to the right place to have luck. Over by the little island west of here might be a good spot; it would be a pleasant boat ride there, anyway."

Andrews turned his head to gaze at her. Doubtless it struck him as a singular coincidence she should speak of the island when he had but come from it.

"I suppose one could fish there as well as anywhere," he said.

"We could have a lot of fun exploring the island even if we caught no fish," the girl continued. "It's said that the place is interesting, with an old, tumble-down house in the middle of the trees and an ancient wreck on the beach. I love mysterious old houses and wrecks. But perhaps you've been to this island so many times, Mr. Andrews, that you're tired of it."

"I've been there," he answered, slowly.

"And is there a wreck on the beach?"

Again the young fellow regarded her with a puzzled face, as Ellen could see by the lamplight from the street falling on Andrews. But there was no suspicion on his countenance.

"Yes, there's a wreck all right," he replied, reluctantly.

"Perhaps it's some old stranded pirate craft."

A faint grin came on his mouth at this romantic idea.

"Its captain might have been an oyster-pirate; that's as near as it ever got to stealing anything, I think. It's just the wreck of an oyster schooner."

"Well, you're going to take me to see it sometime, aren't you?" she asked.

"Yes—sometime."

"When is sometime? That's very indefinite."

"Pretty soon. Some evening——"

"To-morrow evening will suit me nicely; I haven't a thing to keep me and I suppose you'll be free then, too. Shall we plan on going to-morrow evening first thing after supper?"

Andrews stood up suddenly at her words, displaying an odd mixture of consternation and alarm.

"Good Lord, no!" he exclaimed. "I mean—I'll

be busy to-morrow night." He stared down at her
blankly.

"I believe you're afraid. Of ghosts, maybe.
Ghosts are supposed to haunt old wrecks. Of course,
if you're really going to be occupied to-morrow
evening——" Her tone expressed a faint incredu-
lity."

"It's not ghosts, Miss Durand," he stated, vis-
ibly miserable under the sting of her tongue.

"Ah, then it must be that I'm the drawback. I
certainly did not intend to intrude myself into a
boat ride where I was not desired. So if you will
be so kind, we'll consider the subject——"

"Miss Ellen!" Andrews burst out.

"What other inference am I to draw?" she inquired, coldly.

"You know better than that. I'll be glad to take
you to the island sometime, but not to-morrow
night."

Ellen Durand sat still for a moment.

"There's something mysterious about this—and
I do believe you're afraid."

Andrews drew in his breath sharply. Then he
sat down, resting his elbows on his knees and sitting humped over.

"I won't take you there to-morrow evening, that's
all there is about it," he stated, in a sullen tone.
"Think what you please."

"But there must be a reason?"

"Certainly there's a reason—but I'm not going
to tell you what it is," said he, roughly.

Ellen Durand when she had begun the conversation did not know what she would learn; at any rate she had not expected Andrews to announce his visit to the island and to give an explanation of the same; her lead in fact had been rather for the purpose of obtaining some slight information that would enable her to confirm or to disprove his complicity in the plot being hatched by the two foreigners. But now at his obstinacy she felt a wave of anger. It still seemed wholly out of character for him to be a conspirator, and yet his words and secretiveness indicated he was bent on protecting the island from intrusion.

"Oh, well. As you suggest, I shall think what I please," she remarked. "You may rest quite easy as to the future so far as I'm concerned, in the matter of boat rides and everything else; you will not have to take me into consideration in your plans."

Andrews did not look around at her words, or speak. He set his jaw between his palms, elbows on knees, and gazed doggedly towards the street. Two, three minutes passed in silence, while Ellen Durand's resentment was slowly replaced by a growing curiosity as to what queer, vehement, unexpected thoughts filled the other's mind. All at once he expelled a deep breath.

"It doesn't really make any difference what you think or any one thinks after I've gone," he said, in a hard voice. "I've been as good as fired ever since young Stokes came; I got in bad with him

the first day he showed up, and his opinion of me
has grown no better fast; I don't know why he's
kept me hanging on. I'd go to-morrow, only I
first intend to show him he's wrong. When I've
done that, I'll go fast enough."

"You're going somewhere, Mr. Andrews?"

"Yes. To France—that's the place for men like
me. I shall enlist as soon as I'm free here, join
the troops most likely to go over first."

Ellen Durand felt her breath taken by this unexpected declaration.

"You mean you would fight for our side?" she
asked, quickly.

Something near a sniff sounded from Andrews.

"Whom did you suppose I'd fight for? The Germans?" he retorted.

"I was merely wondering."

"Merely wondering!" he exclaimed, without en-
deavoring to conceal a trace of contempt. Then
all at once he dropped his hands and faced about to
scrutinize her. "You seem to have some funny no-
tions in your head about me," he remarked.

"You believe in loyalty then?" she asked.

"Of course."

"To America? To your employers? To your
friends?" Ellen Durand questioned, with deliberate
incisiveness.

The youth leaned forward to peer at her where
she sat in the shadow, his countenance depicting
astonishment or an excellent simulation of such.

"Aren't you feeling well to-night?" he inquired. "Your talk is sort of—well, flighty."

"I'm perfectly well and perfectly calm," was her level response. "I'm merely interested in learning your views in regard to loyalty. You haven't answered my questions."

"Whether I think I should be loyal to America and to Stokes Brothers and all that?"

"Yes."

A new thought appeared to strike the other. His jaw dropped at its adumbration on his brain, but next instant his mouth shut tight.

"Whether I *am* loyal to America and the company, you mean," he exclaimed. "That's what you're trying to learn, isn't that it?"

"It's the same thing," she interjected.

"And you'd like to know whether I'd be a traitor to America, whether I could be bought—by German enemies, say?" he continued, with a hard smile.

"I didn't ask that," she responded weakly, appalled by the embroilment into which her questions had drawn her.

"And what you're really seeking to learn is whether or not I'm loyal to the company and whether or not I've sold out to its enemies," Andrews stated, harshly. "Well, it's quite plain to me now that you suspect, perhaps actually believe, that I have. Maybe Stokes gave you that idea. I wonder if that isn't the reason he has kept me instead of firing me, so he could make sure. Well, I shall stay right on at my job where you both can have your eyes on me all the time, until I am discharged or until matters shape themselves so I can quit and join the army."

He arose, shoved his hands in his trousers' pockets and glared at her defiantly. Ellen Durand also came to her feet.

"Mr. Andrews, I——" she began, hurriedly.

He stopped her with an angry gesture.

"I'm no grandstand hero, understand that," he said, through his teeth, "but nobody can discuss with me my patriotism or loyalty to America and to the company that hires me, or to anything else that has a claim on my allegiance,—and that includes you, Ellen Durand, along with everybody else. You can have Stokes discharge me or arrest me, whichever you please, but you can't insult me to my face by questions of my patriotism and loyalty. I'm a clerk of the company; you and Stokes can give me orders and expect them to be obeyed. If you think I'm a traitor, you know what you can do. But if I answer any questions it will be in a court and not at the hands of any private person who happens to suspect me. I reckon that's enough to say." And without waiting for reply, he marched into the house.

Ellen Durand stood quite motionless for a full minute after the last thump of his feet in mounting the stair within had died away. Had she been less healthy she would have felt ill over the matter; as it was, she suffered a distressing sensation of having unexpectedly bumped her head against a brick wall. She was aware, moreover, that she had converted a friend into an enemy; that alone was enough to upset a person.

"But what was he doing with those men at the old wreck?" she asked herself, finger on cheek.

XV

A NEW CAUSE FOR PERPLEXITY

To Ellen Durand's eager question next morning concerning the police search of the island Bob Stokes shook his head.

"As I feared, the men were gone," he stated. "They had cleaned all of their traps out of the old house and vanished. After a look around through the woods, there was nothing for us to do but come back, as with their big motor boat they could be miles away in any direction seeking a new hole in which to hide. The police will keep a lookout for them, however, for they will be slipping back here again in an attempt to carry out their plans."

"But now they will be more careful and therefore more dangerous than ever," said she.

"So shall we be more careful. I shall increase the number of guards at nights, and have Mulhouse warn our loyal workmen to keep a brighter lookout than ever for trouble and trouble-makers during daytimes. And I shall be ready to grab Andrews at the first sign of new treachery."

The troubled shadow which now always came upon the girl's face when she considered the clerk's mysterious connection with the affair once more rested upon her brow. Stokes observed her with a pang of jealousy stirring in his mind at her persistent and unreasonable belief in Andrews' honesty. Though at this moment she said nothing, he felt that she still somehow was unconvinced of the young fellow's disloyal part in the plot, despite his presence on the island last night; was unconvinced because of some latent bit of stubbornness or some mistaken intuition, or possibly because of a simple generosity of heart which could not accept a one-time trusted acquaintance's infamy as an actual fact.

"If these suspicions had fallen upon Mr. Mocket instead of Mr. Andrews, queer as it may seem to you, I should have believed them the sooner," she remarked at last, musingly.

Stokes thrust his hands into his pockets and stared at her.

"Of all extraordinary things, why?" he exclaimed.

"Well, I can't give a really satisfactory explanation, in fact, can only say that I don't like Mr. Mocket and never have liked him from the first day. There is something about the man——"

"Has he ever been uncivil to you, or presuming?" Bob interrupted quickly, taking a step towards her.

"No, Mr. Stokes. Never in a single instance. He's always perfectly polite and if anything reserved; in fact, he has always kept to himself and to his work, displaying no interest whatever in me or my duties. I appreciate that on his part. But—and perhaps I shouldn't speak of it—he repels me notwithstanding his respectful manner. For all his subdued air and quiet bearing and look of integrity, I dislike the man and somehow distrust him. The feeling has grown on me of late; his eyes behind their glasses seem to know too much and at moments appear to be even mocking. It's only an intuition, a shadowy something I can't define, but it is very strong. And I haven't in the least such a feeling for Mr. Andrews,—no, not even after last night's happening."

"Intuitions aren't always reliable," Bob answered.

"I know—but women depend upon them a great deal. There's something else too; it flashed into my mind one day that Mr. Mocket wasn't a native American. So I asked him and he answered that he was born in New York; but I felt as he spoke and as he looked at me that his words were not true. If you've ever noticed closely, his English while perfect is at times a little precise, as if it had been learned instead of unconsciously acquired —well, with his baby teeth, say. And there is a slight foreign cast to his features."

"So great a part of our population isn't native American that even many born here may have such a look," he said.

"It may all be moonshine of mine, Mr. Stokes, but I'll confess that I've wondered——"

She broke off as if in finishing the sentence she

might be committing herself too far to her suspicions.

"Please continue," Bob said. "What you say will be kept in confidence."

"Well, I've wondered if he had anything to do with betraying your interests. For one thing, he's a far more capable man than Mr. Andrews, who is more energetic than subtle; a man, I think, who would be much better qualified than Mr. Andrews to direct a plot."

"Andrews isn't directing it; he simply acts under orders from some one else who provides the brains," Bob stated.

"Perhaps I've become so nervous over everything that I've taken to suspecting the wrong persons. It is true, Mr. Mocket has never once given me real grounds for believing him anything but what he appears to be."

"Don't imagine I haven't given serious attention to what you say," he replied. "For I have, and I shall consider your suggestion again. But hard facts alone can lead us to the conspirators; a good many facts at present throw a bad light on Andrews. I'll take a good look at Mocket, mark his enunciation and so on, however. We can't afford to overlook any possibility that may reveal the plotters, or assume that the cashier or any one else is beyond proof of complicity."

Stokes proceeded in this particular matter with promptitude. In the course of the next half hour he called the man in for a conference in respect to certain financial items and during their talk took occasion to study Mocket's lineaments, features and general countenance as well as his utterance. When he finally dismissed the cashier, he began thoughtfully to pace the floor.

Ellen Durand had been right. About the man's speech there was, when one marked it closely, a suggestion of unnaturalness, or rather as she had said of preciseness, and once or twice Bob had perceived a tendency on Mocket's part to shave a "w" into a "v," which under ordinary circumstances Stokes would never have perceived. About the man's face, and his thin figure, too, was an illusive hint of an alien race strain. But of what race? His name bespoke English blood, at least. Yet what of the clipped "w"? After all could the man be a Teuton?

The thought seemed preposterous. All the deductions were vague and unsubstantial. Still Stokes had a feeling—yes, he must admit it—a feeling similar to that asserted by Ellen Durand; a sensed apprehension that Mocket was different from what he appeared on the surface; that he left an impression of restrained and concealed force, of hardness and carefully veiled contempt and distrust. The man's eyes in fact had glowed in a way his glasses could not altogether obscure, as if within him burned some deep, secret, consuming fire which was not elsewhere revealed upon his thin, severe countenance. Truth was, Bob Stokes was exceed-

ingly perplexed while at the same time moved by
unaccountable misgivings.

"I wonder, Miss Durand, if such a thing is possible as Mocket and Andrews working together for
the company's betrayal," he said, finally.

"They have never by their actions shown any
secret understanding between themselves, or for
that matter manifested any intimacy," she responded.

"That may be only a precaution to throw others
off their guard."

But she shook her head at this suggestion.

"Mr. Andrews doesn't like Mr. Mocket, I know.
He's never said so outright, but he has unconsciously shown that he dislikes the man. But if Mr. Andrews is guilty, that doesn't amount to anything,
does it? I'll confess that so many things have happened that my reason tells me in spite of my intuition, when I think them over, he must be associated with the plotters. And the thought frightens
me."

"You mustn't allow it to do that; we shall take
care of Andrews, and Mocket, too, if he be implicated, all in good time."

"It makes me tremble to think those men may
be criminals. The truth is there are some things
more I know that I've never told you. To-night
I'll study the whole matter over and then to-morrow
perhaps give you this information. First, I want
to be certain I'm justified, though."

"I'll not press you to tell me anything against

your desire. But there is a great deal involved—
our business, our ships, and possibly men's lives."

"Nothing shall be kept back you should know,"
she answered, with anxiety sounding in her voice.
"I want to set everything clear in my own mind
first, however."

Her distress over what occupied her thoughts was
so evident that Bob Stokes decided it wise to let
the subject rest, leaving her to reach a decision in
her own good time. As he had occasion to go forth
into the yard he therefore took up his hat and left
the building, giving the two men in the outer office
a sharp glance as he passed through. But both were
industriously engaged at accustomed tasks; Andrews checking over bills as virtuously as the most
honest clerk in the world, and as if he knew nothing about any island, or wreck, or secret meeting
with strangers, or wooden case of dynamite last
night hidden in the old hulk; Mocket footing accounts calmly and carefully, his black coat and
spare figure as respectable as a clergyman's, his
thin ascetic face bent in attention to his page.

"You would never guess from them we were all
sitting on gun-powder," Stokes remarked to himself, when he was in the open.

In the yard the huge hulls of the building vessels dominated the scene. As he moved forward
along the length of the one nearing completion, with
workmen busy about it, with the ceaseless signs and
sounds of toil on every hand, his heart swelled with
the exultation of a great task being carried through,

and with a fresh determination to thwart the company's enemies, crush them, and safely launch these future stout merchantmen of the sea.

In imagination he beheld the ships with all sail set driving ahead through the ocean, bearing their burdens of freight and in a degree serving mankind. Riders of the great waters, servants of nations! And he was moved by a profound feeling that into these wooden shapes went something more than a mere hope of commercial gain—something good, noble and sublime; the unconscious contribution of spirit of a multitude of faithful patriotic men.

The thought was to him an inspiration and an encouraging force. The fact that these boats were being constructed against obstacles and in spite of treacherous attacks made them but the more precious. They were moreover typical of what Americans could do in an emergency when the world shipping was threatened; and that was to him a source of keen pride. And in a way the ships were symbolic, too! Symbolic of the nation's new merchant marine, of the vast fleet of vessels as yet shadowy but which was beginning to rise everywhere along our shores; of the fleet that was again to bring back the ship supremacy of the United States of a century before, that was to revive and restore our flag upon the seven seas, that should once more in shipping make us independent of the world. A vast fleet rising out of the mists to greet

the sun! Ships rising from a dream into a reality!
Ships resurgent!

Bob Stokes, thrilled by the conception, pulled off
his hat and stood bare of head beside the building
ship, gazing reverently into space as a vision.

XVI

SNOHOMISH JIM PLAYS A CARD

ABOUT nine o'clock of the evening, two nights after Bob Stokes had led half a dozen of Martinsport's police force to the island, only to find their game flown, Snohomish Jim sat with two cronies in a stuffy little room at the rear of an old, tumbledown, wooden store building on a back street. A rickety outside stair rising from the alley led up to the second floor where it was located. Sections of the plastering were missing, revealing the lath. A scurry and squeak of rats could at times be heard under the flooring. The windows were boarded up. The only furniture of the room was several boxes used for seats and a grimy table bearing a smoky lamp and three partly emptied pint bottles of whiskey, one to the hand of each of the three men sitting about the light.

"And if he gives me much more of his lip," one of Jim's companions was saying, a man with a lined, red-patched, evil face and the forefinger gone from his left hand, "if he gives me much more of his dirty lip, I say, I'll hit him behind the ear with a piece of pipe some night." He paused to mouth a string of curses. "We're pulling our freight,

189

Pete here and me, pretty quick anyway—when we've got a little more easy money."

His present grievance was directed against Bob Stokes, who had come on him loafing at work and ordered him to get busy or to get his time. The man had chosen the former alternative. But hence the threatened retaliation.

"Good luck to you, boys," said Jim, reaching over and giving each of the men a hearty clap on the shoulder. "You're men after my own ideas, with no nonsense about you and with spirit. This is no place for fellers like us—I'm beating it myself when I've got some traveling coin. You say you're going when you've got a handful of easy money—but I ain't seen any easy money around here. That's why I'm moving on, where there's a chance to do a little quiet job for good pay. Why, a feller slipped me a hundred once for just sticking a piece of dynamite under a freight car! Nothing like that around here. I'm going north where the money grows. Here's to better days for all of us!"

He thrust the mouth of the bottle between his lips and gulped down a swallow of the fiery liquor. The others did likewise.

"Better days it is," said the third of the trio, setting down his bottle and wiping his mustache with the back of his hand. He relighted his cigar and turned his bloodshot eyes on Snohomish Jim. "Where you heading for?" he asked.

"Them munition towns," said Jim. "There's

strikes and labor wars going on there, they say. That's my meat. Always a chance to pick up a bank-roll for easy work." He lolled back in his chair and snapped his big fingers. "I asks no questions when some boy pushes me a bunch of bills and names his job. We workingmen are ground down by the capitalists and so got to grab easy money to be even. We're getting only what's coming to us, say I. Blow the rich men to hell, too! The capitalists put me in the pen for five years at hard labor, wearing their dirty stripes, and I'm for dynamite and the red flag now, boys!"

Snohomish Jim pounded the table with his huge fist and smacked his lips. He looked quite as evil and infinitely more ferocious than his mates.

"What's the matter with Jack and me going along with you?" Pete inquired.

"Sure. You're the right sort of pals for any feller, you and Jack." He laid an arm about the latter's shoulder. "We'll go north together and turn a trick for big money and live easy for a month, lads. Plenty of grub and booze and girls. Plenty of fun—and no morning whistle! Heh, Jack?"

"I'm on," said Jack. And he sang a line of a ribald song. Then he raised his bottle, exclaiming, "Drink hearty, men." He drained the flask and cast it on the floor. "I'll call Markham to bring another, the old thief!"

As he arose and went towards the hallway, Jim called him back.

"Your money's made of tin, you lop-eared hel-

lion! Sit down and go to that." He drew a fresh
pint flask from his hip and tossed it on the table,
then hoarsely chanted, " 'It kicks a man at twenty
rods, it kills at forty-nine'——"

"When'll we go?" asked Jack, seating himself.

"To-morrow—or next day. When I get my time
at the shipyard, I'll have enough for a ticket,"
Jim said.

Pete looked significantly at Jack.

"We got that job," said he.

"Aw, let 'er go. You ain't tied to building ships,"
said Jim.

"This ain't ships—and it gives us a roll."

"Why don't I get in on it, then?" Jim demanded.
"I don't hang round waiting for you fellers, with
big money up north, unless I make something. And
you want some of that coin that's flowing up in
them munition towns, don't you? A thousand dollars a job, maybe two or three thousand, if it's
dynamite work—and you can write it down in your
little book I'm there with the dynamite goods."

Pete's face lighted with greed. His fingers opened
and closed.

"You're our pal; so we've a right to our split
out of it," he said.

Jim's air grew peevish. He took a drink from
his bottle, frowned, swore an oath or two.

"Then what we waiting for?" he asked.

"For the easy money we got coming first," said
Pete.

"I don't see none."

Jack pushed his hat on one side.

"What's the matter with taking Jim in and making him come across with more cash?" he questioned Pete.

"Him" did not refer to Snohomish Jim; "him" pertained to some person unnamed, to whom Jack and Pete had engaged their services at private hire. The big woodman's eyes gleamed at the word.

"Maybe we can—and Jim here knows about using the stuff," was the answer.

"What stuff?" Jim demanded.

"Powder, dynamite."

"Sure I do! Used to shoot rock in Alaska—'fore that, in Africa. Slept with my head on a box of dynamite. I'm an expert." He gave a wave of his hand, as if the fact were quite beyond question. "I can fix a charge that wouldn't more'n blow a knot out of a knot-hole, or that would send every stick of Stokes' ships to hell. That's me. Used to shoot off a pinch in my hair for a hair-cut when the barber wasn't around. All in knowing how to handle it. Don't let the booze spoil, boys—they're making more all the time, too. What's he paying for this job?"

They drank. When Jim had wiped his lips and long mustache, he repeated the question.

"Two hundred dollars," said Pete.

A snort came from Jim.

"Ought to be more. When do you pull it off?"

"He's to let us know—day or two, maybe. Week, maybe. Waiting for the right night, he says."

Snohomish Jim appeared to meditate. Finally he laid a hand on the shoulder of each and drew the men nearer.

"You're getting a hundred apiece—tell him you need me to help," said he, "and stick up the price to five hundred. He won't have time to get other men now, and he'll dig up the coin. That means traveling money for us, pals. We'll blow away up north with the cash in our pockets. Make him pay for his fun. Five hundred; that amounts to more'n one-sixty each feller of us, so you see I'm making you money right at the jump. And when we're up in them munition towns, take it from me, boys, we'll clean up a roll as big as your leg! Tell this feller here it's five hundred or no go; tell him you've studied it over and it's a three-man job; tell him we got to have the cash the morning of the work, or we don't shoot a stick, for we must plan to travel fast and light when the celebration's over. D'you get me?"

Apparently they did. The prospect of an increase in the remuneration for their services fired their imaginations exactly as the whiskey heated their blood.

"If he don't pay five hundred, we'll smash his dirty head," said Jack. "You're a square pal, Jim, and I seen it the first drink we ever took together." He swayed a little in his chair. "I says to Pete then, 'That guy's all there and square.'"

Pete was occupied by another thought.

"He ought to have paid more for them jobs we

done already," he stated, in a sullen tone. "And we had to split with other fellers we got to do things we couldn't tend to."

"What did they do?" Jim questioned.

"Nothing but kick in with the bad work," was the disgusted reply.

"They was mostly caught and fired," said Jack.

"Well, this feller who's hiring us has got to pay five hundred, or we quit," said Jim. "And why not tell him so immediate? If this job—what is it, Stokes' boats?—is going to be pulled off maybe in a couple of days, then we got to have the cash in our pockets right off. Business first, that's me. And what's the use of waiting, boys? We're doing the job, we ought to have the say-so when. Tell him to-night. Let him pay us to-morrow; we'll pack in the stuff in our dinner-pails——"

"He says that he'll have bombs we can throw," said Jack. "Ain't that what he told you, Pete?"

"Yes."

"Let 'er go bombs, then. And we'll hide in the yard at quitting time till dark, shoot, beat it and hop a train for them munition towns. Do you do the talking with him, Pete? Well, round him up to-night and tell him what's what. To-morrow this time we'll be traveling north with five hundred and our wages in our pants. And then the bright lights for us, lads. Pass round that bottle, Jack, till we kill it." The flask passed from hand to hand, until Pete gulped down the last inch of liquor and flung the bottle into a corner.

"I'll telephone him I want to see him right away," he said, jumping to his feet.

"Go to it, Pete, you're the feller to make him come across," Jim exclaimed.

They tramped out of the room, leaving the smoky lamp on the table behind them, and passed down the rickety stair into the alley. Coming forth upon a side street, they entered a cheap night restaurant, where Pete presently obtaining a telephone connection proceeded to hold a guarded conversation

"Hamburger steak and coffee for three, you black ape," he ordered the negro behind the counter, when through his colloquy. Then addressing his companions, said, "Meets me in half an hour at his house, so we'll eat till then. Says I got to see him alone, like I always have."

"Tell him I'm your brother, who usually works with you and has just come to town," said Jim. "A feller can't kick much against a man's only brother."

Jim guffawed, with the other pair joining in the laugh. The restaurant was empty of eaters except for themselves, as its patrons had not yet begun to drop in, so they had nothing to fear by being overheard.

"How long will you be gone?" Jack asked of his comrade.

"Don't know. Maybe an hour, I guess. He doesn't like to give up coin, but I'll make him head in."

The negro appeared and slid their meal on the counter before them, whereupon they fell to consuming the hamburger and fried potatoes with gusto. When they had finished, Jim said:

"Well, I'm going to bed and I'll see you in the morning. Keep the screws on him, boy, till he says he'll pay."

"I'm hungry yet; stick around, Jim," Jack said. With an oath he ordered the negro to cook him a plate of eggs.

But Jim wanted no more food. Outside the door he again told Pete to make "him" agree to pay five hundred, then the two men separated.

XVII

A SECRET CONFERENCE

Jim Flanagan strode along the dimly lighted pavement, keeping an eye over his shoulder in order to follow the movements of the man from whom he had just parted. He perceived Pete arrive at an intersection of the street, turn the corner. Instantly Jim pivoted about and set out to follow him.

Had he acted on his natural inclination while in the boot-legger's back room over the alley, he would have seized the two scoundrels by their throats and then and there made settlement for the injury inflicted upon Frederic Stokes. His long fingers itched to smash their heads together. He had been in Stokes Brothers' employ for ten years and friendship as well as hire and work was represented by that period. Loyalty was his dominant feeling. But his native coolness, which at all times prevailed, directed his actions in order that he might discover the chief conspirator and serve the greater interests of his firm by getting, so to speak, the man's head into a bag. The active tools, Pete and Jack, should receive their deserts later.

He rounded the corner and observed Pete slouching ahead, something less than a block in front. The pursuit led across the main business street, then out of the business section altogether and into a residence district at the extreme edge of town given over to workingmen's and truck gardener's cottages separated from each other by vacant ground. Jim found it necessary to fall even farther back behind the man he trailed, for they were now the only pedestrians on the street, the householders of the quarter apparently being in bed. As an added precaution against any betrayal by sound he slipped off his boots to carry under his arm. He could see Pete at regular intervals when the latter passed under successive gas lamps.

Under one, finally, the fellow halted to consult his watch, afterwards looking back and to all appearances listening. Then, as if assured all was well he proceeded on his errand while Jim sprang through the weeds bordering the walk out into the road. The latter with long strides lessened the space between his quarry and himself until he could hear the other's footsteps on the cement walk. Pete was now barely fifty paces in advance.

All at once the man turned in at a small dwelling with no near neighbor and showing no light. A few pines stood about the dim structure, left uncut when the ground had been cleared, whose thick boughs intensified the gloom. The silence was broken only by faint sounds from the city. Jim, harking in the road, heard Pete's feet ascend a small porch, next heard a low interchange of words, and finally the closing of a door.

The time consumed had been considerably more than the half hour set to lapse for the meeting, but the unknown had nevertheless awaited Pete's tardy arrival. Isolated as it was, the house was well placed for a secret conference—Jim could smell garden patches all about. A peaceful neighborhood! One wouldn't suspect anything doing here! He cocked an ear for a minute towards the house, then advanced without sound.

Reaching the porch he listened again. He finally moved round a corner of the dwelling, guiding himself with a hand on the weatherboarding until his fingers encountered a window ledge. A murmur of voices proceeded from inside. Once there came a slight flare as from a lighted match, which illuminated the window panes. The men were talking in the dark and one of them, probably Pete, was smoking. Snohomish Jim placed his boots on the grass by the house, squatted himself down producing a plug of tobacco from which he bit off a liberal piece, and thus prepared to conduct his watch in comfort.

Occasionally the voices rose in pitch. The men were in altercation over the matter of the five hundred dollars and the new recruit. Jim grinned to himself. He could even make out, he thought, Pete's hoarse tones. He munched his tobacco and listened and meditated.

Suddenly an indistinct sound caused him to prick up his ears. Then he noiselessly let himself down upon hands and knees. Some one was moving in his direction along the side of the house; his acute hearing distinguished the soft brush of feet on the grass. Once he thought he glimpsed a vague form stealing towards him from the rear of the building, hugging its side. When a few feet away, the new visitor paused and Flanagan heard him expel a long breath. After a minute he came on, his finger-tips giving forth a gentle rubbing sound on the side of the house as he moved.

Just at the second he was about to collide with the woodsman, Snohomish Jim arose like a shadow before the man. His long arms shot out, his hands closed about the other's neck, a big thumb shut off the unknown's windpipe, while a foot kicked out the man's legs from under him. The whole operation was executed neatly and without scuffle. For a little the prisoner, his head jammed down on Flanagan's boots, fought desperately to free himself, but Jim pressed him flat with his own weight.

"Don't you peep, if you want to breathe," Jim hissed. "I'm going to let you have air now, but if you open your mouth to make a sound it'll be good-night for you; I'll break your neck."

At the release of his thumb, the victim gasped with painful suspirations until his breathing once more became normal. Jim still retained a palm about his neck, but with the other hand produced a match, ignited it against his knee and keeping it shielded held the flame to his captive's face. After a scrutiny he blew out the light.

"Well, boy, I've got your number," said he in a

whisper. "You're the cub in the office at the ship-yard. What you doing here?" And when the other continued silent, he added, "Come through, if you don't want me to shut off your talking apparatus for good. Say it quiet and careful, too."

"Trying to learn what these men are doing here."

"Then you ain't one of 'em?"

"No."

"You on the side of the Stokes?"

"Yes."

"No lies now, or I'll tear your head off."

"I'm not lying," was the vigorous assertion, "and I'm not a dirty traitor to the men that hire me! If you're against them, I'll say the same anyway!"

Jim lifted his body off his prisoner.

"That's one mark to the good for you—and not so loud!" he ordered. "Now sit up. But I'm keeping a hand on you, so no breaks. I'll look you over again later on."

His prisoner availed himself of the privilege. He said nothing for a time, but appeared to be rubbing his throat.

"Where are they? I was trying to locate them when you grabbed me," he whispered, presently.

"Inside here. But I can't hear what they say. Got to sit tight."

"Well, who are you? My name's Andrews."

"Call me Jim, boy, just call me Jim. That's what they call me to breakfast by. Know what these fellers are up to?"

"No."

"How did you get here then?"

"Followed the first man. Laid low while he sat on the porch until the other feller came. When they went inside, I moved round the house to find a way inside if I could."

The conversation continued in whispers. The pair sat in the angle formed by the house and the earth, the figure of each just visible to the other. Jim at this stage removed the hand which had been kept in precaution on Andrews' shoulder.

"How did you come to follow the man in the first place?" he asked.

"Been watching him. Wanted to find out who's responsible for what's been happening in the yard. After Mr. Stokes was nailed with that plank, I knew somebody was out to do the company up. So I got busy."

"Who's this feller you trailed?"

"He works in the yard," Andrews answered, non-committally.

"Learn anything about him?"

To this question the youth made no immediate response. He peered at his companion in an endeavor to make out his lineaments. Figuratively as well as literally he was talking in the dark.

"Say, you Jim, supposing you loosen up some," he said. "I'm not giving up everything I know. You might be out to do the company yourself, for all I can tell. Who the devil are you, anyway?"

A reassuring pat on the back met this query.

"There, boy, there. I'm guard-deen of the

Stokes family and raised 'em from the bottle, almost," Jim stated.

"I guess you're pulling for them, if that's the case."

"All the time, including nights and Sundays. I'm trailing the crooks myself and got here by covering the second feller. Whoever starts a fire in the Stokes' timber finds Jim Flanagan loping through the sticks after him, with both hands open."

Andrews grunted.

"They're some hands too," said he.

"You didn't get any real feel out of 'em, boy, I handled you tender and reserved-like, observing you didn't have any heft to speak of. You ought to swing an ax for a few years." After a pause, he remarked, "Doesn't the man you followed live here?"

"No, I don't believe any one does," Andrews replied.

Snohomish Jim reflected upon this fact. It indicated that the crooks' employer was using it as a rendezvous to prevent Pete from learning his true domicile. It might indicate that Pete did not know in the least who the man was, and never had seen his face, if the meetings had all been conducted thus in the dark house. Learning that Pete was a suitable tool, the chief plotter could have arranged indirectly for a first meeting here and engaged him and his mate to do his criminal work. If the men were too curious regarding his identity, they could learn nothing from the house; if they disclosed

the nature of the plot, his face remained unknown
to them. He doubtless used a false name. He might
have a key to the house with no authority whatever,
using the dwelling for his night conferences without the owner's knowledge. That would not be a
difficult trick to turn in an empty abode in this lone-
some part of the city. The fellow had covered his
tracks like a fox.

But this boy Andrews knew who he was!

"Have you been here before?" he questioned.

"No. He headed out this way one night last
week, but I was too far back. I didn't see where
he turned in and lost him. It was only after Mr.
Stokes was hurt that I took to watching where he
went, though I'd begun to be suspicious before."

"What's his name?"

Andrews shifted his position on the ground.

"Well, I'm not saying till I get the goods on him,
if he's guilty. No need of naming names yet."

"All right, boy," said Jim. "Glad to see you
don't spout, anyway. That's something. Most fellers shoot off their mouths too much as it is. Play
your cards close to your vest till the bets are all in,
then play 'em hard. That's me! So you run out
your string and I'll follow mine and maybe we'll
meet up at the end."

"But I'll say this much; I don't think my man's
the head of the scheme. There's another higher up
—and a big man," Andrews asserted.

"Then that's where the bank-roll is," said Jim.

"Wouldn't be surprised. But my suspicion isn't

more than a suspicion. I followed my man several times to an office, the office of this other gentleman, when no one was wise I was around. Wasn't supposed to be away from work myself. Took a chance, however. I wanted to know where he went, and then when I learned where he was going, I wondered why he was visiting this rich man. By asking quiet questions I discovered he had worked for the big sport before coming to the Stokes Company, though he had always kept mum about it. He's been to see him several times in the last ten days. Then he called him up once—I looked up the number afterwards—when he thought I was busy. Said, 'Matters are progressing.' That was straight after a string of cars was derailed by a spiked switch. It sounded mighty queer, coming on top of the accident. And I asked myself what business he had reporting anything to anybody outside the office, anyway. Stokes Brothers pay him his salary."

"Right-o!"

"Well, that's all, but I'm betting my job that if money's being spent by this man in the house here, I know who's putting it up," Andrews declared.

"It's being spent. They're arguing a five hundred dollar deal in there now, lad."

Andrews drew a deep breath.

"Then Main's putting up—that settles it!" Andrews exclaimed inadvertently.

"And who's this guy Main?" Jim asked.

"One of the half dozen rich men in Martinsport.

You might as well know, since I've said his name. Owns most of the gas company. 'Gas' Main, they call him. Big walloper. Put a crimp in a strike last summer when he reduced wages, by importing a bunch of thugs who beat up a dozen workmen to an inch of their lives. The town's small, so the strike petered out. Not big enough to fight back."

"What's he got to do with the Stokes?"

"Now you're asking something. If I knew, the whole rotten scheme would be plain," Andrews answered. "That's what I'm anxious to find out, but it's not likely I shall."

"Boy, you forget Jim Flanagan is out for bear," that worthy stated. "When I line my traps, I always bring home bear meat. If this 'Gas' Main is prowling in Stokes' tract, he's going to be snapped by the foot and then fried in a pan. Part your hair by that, Andy, part your hair by that."

Whether or not he would do so, Andrews failed to announce. The sudden opening of the door at the front of the house and a sound of voices upon the porch interrupted their colloquy. Pete and his companion had come forth. Flanagan, with Andrews on his hands and knees behind him, crept cautiously forward until within earshot.

"I've conceded your demand in regard to your brother and the money, but to-morrow night is too soon," said he whose tones were unknown to Jim. "Perhaps in two or three days; I'm as desirous of having the affair concluded as you are. But I reserve the right to say when."

"Well, we can't hang round forever," Pete growled.

"You're getting good pay and doubly so now that I've raised the amount," the other answered. "One of you had better stop work and remain where I can get in touch with you any minute. At your boarding-house, say. I may know by Monday."

"We'll all quit work at noon Monday then and be ready," Pete answered.

A moment's silence ensued.

"Very well. And you'd better leave the whiskey alone till you're through. I want you sober when the time comes. If you're drunk——"

"Who's going to be drunk? Don't preach to me."

"See that you are sober, then. And now, don't attempt to call me up for another meeting like this, for I expect to be occupied every minute hereafter until the thing comes off. I'll not return to this house again. Are you sure you can trust your brother?"

"Huh. With my last dime! No squarer feller ever lived than Jim, barring none." Pete's eulogy was uttered with a vigor that delighted one hearer.

"Very well."

"What about the bombs? Do you bring 'em to us?" was the inquiry.

"No. I explained that before. They will be ready at the yard; you'll receive them there. I'm taking no chance on any one stumbling on them in your possession. All that's necessary for you and the others to do is to follow my instructions, be at the right place at the right time and do the work."

Pete sniffed.

"And all you have to do is to have the bundle of cash in our hands by evening that day," said he, "we'll do the rest."

"It will be delivered in a package to you at your hotel by a messenger boy, who'll take a receipt. And now, a last word. To make sure that you show up, there'll be another hundred for you personally when I meet you in the yard."

The listeners heard Pete give a step forward in surprise.

"What's that!" he exclaimed.

"Another hundred for you personally, I said."

A grunt of pleasure escaped the hireling.

"Mr. Smith, you're as fair and square a man as ever I done business with," Pete asserted heartily. "I never hope to see a squarer. We'll do your job for you quick and handsome, especially since we got Jim now, and you can figure on us as true pals. There'll be sticks falling all over town, so you better have your umbreller." And Pete broke into a jocose laugh.

"Well, that's all for to-night. I'll not keep you longer," said the other.

"All right, I'll hit it for town. Sleep merry, boss."

Pete descended the steps and set off.

"Remember to quit work and await word from me," was sent after him.

"Sure. We'll be ready."

Thereupon Pete proceeded on his way. After a time a cheerful whistle came back to the others, dying with distance as his footsteps diminished. Pete had picked up a hundred dollars more of easy money; his heart was light.

On the grass at the end of the porch Snohomish Jim and Andrews lay unstirring, still as the darkness itself. The man who had stayed behind continued to stand where Pete had left him, apparently listening until assured that his tool had really departed. For five minutes after Pete's last footstep had stopped he waited, then he himself went down and away.

Jim and Andrews drew themselves to their knees.

"Well, I've rested my feet, anyway—that's something," said Snohomish Jim. "Always like to give my corns a chance. Wait till I get my boots."

XVIII

WHICH HAS NOTHING TO DO WITH SHIPS

AN unexplainable restlessness, a desire to escape for a brief period from the strain of warding off secret enemies of the company and safeguarding the property and to enjoy a free light-hearted hour, and a yearning for companionship, too, resulted Sunday in Bob Stokes telephoning Ellen Durand proposing an automobile ride into the country for the afternoon. In a state of suspense more than he would have admitted even to himself he awaited her answer, and experienced a huge relief and quick pleasure when after a meditative pause she announced she would be glad to go. At about three o'clock therefore they were riding at leisurely speed along a road through the pine woods lying north of Martinsport.

On either side arose the thick timber, with the soft languid sunshine playing among the tops of the tall straight pines and dropping beams even into half-hidden marshy spots marked by a riotous growth of ground palms, vivid green vines and underbrush. The air was scented by a pungent woodsy odor. An occasional bird glanced soundlessly across the open roadway. At intervals when they passed some old untenanted cabin in a clearing or a worked-out abandoned turpentine camp, the lazy silence and solitude of the woods seemed the more profound.

"Restful, isn't it?" Stokes said. "There's nothing like getting away from people into timber land to clear one's brain of vapors and fill it with ozone. There's something eminently sane about trees—in spite of the fact that men have sometimes grown queer from living too long alone in the woods."

"I love to come into the woods at times, but I'm afraid I should grow queer too if compelled to live in a forest a long time at a stretch. Five years, say," Ellen responded.

Stokes smiled.

"Who wouldn't? A healthy normal person doesn't need or want solitude. If one is busy at work in the timber, why, that's different; and even so, there's always a reaction when one has been away from civilized society too long. That explains, and perhaps excuses, the 'tears' lumber-jacks and loggers go on when they hit town after several months' absence. Too much 'solitude' in their systems. But it's good to get out for a few hours like this and smell bark once more."

"Yes, indeed."

"But I prefer to do it as I'm doing it now. With another," he remarked, looking about at her and smiling again.

Her eyelashes fluttered the barest trifle, while involuntarily she drew in a quick breath. She glanced aside at the trees lining the roadside and slightly averted her face in fear lest unbidden color were rising there.

"I think every one does who isn't melancholy—and you certainly are not that."

Her composure suddenly returned at the words; she faced him as if to scrutinize his countenance for any possible trace of gloom. Then she shook her head and continued:

"I don't believe you're the sort of man who would ever be melancholy under any circumstances. For that matter, I don't imagine I ever should be; I can be sad, or angry, or stubborn, or perhaps even revengeful, though I'm not sure, but I could never sink into a state of morbid despondency."

"You have too much spirit," Bob said. "The thing that interested my brother in Seattle and me when your telegrams first came was your spirit. Fighting spirit too, I call it."

A soft laugh came from Ellen's lips.

"Do I look like a fighter?" she questioned.

"You look—your sweet self."

The words slipped from his lips without conscious intent on his part, or volition. And then as he realized they were uttered a little throb of passion began to beat in his breast, and he knew they were exactly what he had been wanting to say without daring.

"I suppose that means I don't look belligerent," she stated, presently. "However much fighting spirit I may have, I don't care to appear as anything more than a girl, as girls usually are."

Her dark eyes, with their dusky glow of light, consulted his.

"Not many who came to know you would class you with the ordinary run of girls, I imagine," Bob returned, emphatically. "Why, you're a hundred times more intelligent, and interesting, and—well, alive. You are——"

Ellen Durand checked what more he was about to say. She was laughing and blushing too in confusion, for her companion's speech was decidedly earnest.

"See where you're driving the car! Nearly off the road into a tree!" she exclaimed. "I'm enjoying your flattering description of myself, but I don't want it at the risk of my neck. You weren't watching the way at all."

Bob steered the car back into the middle of the road, without experiencing any particular distress over the circumstance of his heedlessness.

"Here's a track branching off west; we'll try it and see where it leads. But everything I said was true," he remarked.

And truly to the young fellow she was all and more than he had asserted. Essentially feminine, she possessed in marked degree the qualities that distinguish and attract: an abundant health, youth and an ardent eagerness to adventure on life, an independence and quickness of mind, an instinctive sympathy of soul, and that haunting element of mystery which both defeats and charms man. In the depths of her eyes seemed to lurk thoughts Bob Stokes could not plumb or guess, and indeed suggested possibilities of passion and resolve and sacrifice of which she herself did not dream. Who, in sooth, can measure the profound forces of which a rich, full and pulsing nature is capable?

"Do you know where this road leads?" she asked, after a time.

"I haven't the least idea," he replied.

"Then we're exploring."

"Yes."

"So much the better; the unexpected may lie just around a curve," she stated. "Some people want always to keep to the road they know, for fear something may happen or they may become lost. What is so dreadful about being lost?"

"Not a thing, except in the person's mind," Bob answered promptly. "One need never be lost, you know, if one keep his or her mind cool, though in a place one has never been before or knows nothing about. There's always a path out and home. Prospectors go over hundreds of miles never traveled before and are not lost. Timber cruisers plunge into forests they've never seen before and aren't lost. A person is never lost anywhere—until his coolness of mind is lost and he grows frightened. All that it is necessary to do when one becomes bewildered in an unknown place is to halt, keep calm, observe the signs, such as the direction of the sun and of streams and a few other pointers given by nature, and set one's self straight, then move out according to the signs."

"That sounds simple, but is it?" And then she added, "I believe I should keep cool, even if I was frightened. And I should not be frightened long; as I said, there's really nothing dreadful about becoming lost, unless one were a long way from people and water and food. The uncertainty would give the experience a zest."

"And you talk of going to New York? You were made to live on the frontier," Bob exclaimed.

"Ah, not live there! A taste of the wilderness might be exciting but it would not satisfy. People—the millions of people in a great city—make the real wilderness for one to—what shall I say,—prospect and cruise in, and perhaps find treasure and perhaps not, but in any case have the joy of searching."

"For what?" was the brief question.

"For——" Ellen Durand paused, sitting in consideration. "For happiness, I suppose, most of all. For knowledge and experience and wisdom and love, and happiness in the end."

"I didn't know New York or any other large city had a monopoly of those things," he said, a smile hovering on his lips.

"Oh, they haven't, of course."

"I doubt if the average person there, living in the turmoil he does, has as much happiness as one living away. As for knowledge, it depends on what you mean by the words. Experience—of a particular, limited kind, yes. Wisdom? Rather sharp-

ness. And so far as love is concerned, no less probably, no more certainly, for so far as I've ever
heard love happens anywhere and everywhere without regard to surroundings, in New York and in a
desert—and in Martinsport. Same with happiness.
One's a state of heart and the other a state of
mind, and not the State of New York or the city
either, isn't that so?"

Ellen Durand shook her head.

"I only know that I've been starved for friends
and happiness and contentment here," said she, "so
I'm ready to try somewhere else. Perhaps it's just
the glamor of a big city——"

"That's it partly, I fancy," Bob interjected.

"But that's something; Martinsport hasn't even
that."

The young fellow beside her felt himself combat-
ing a force vague, intangible, illusive, just what
he could not say. Unexpressed desires and long-
ings and dreams perhaps, shadowy hopes and stifled
aspirations. It was as if he beheld her with arms
reaching forth for what he could not see. And
he felt himself perplexed and baffled, while a feeling like jealousy stirred within his breast at this
formless thing which drew her away.

"You're so terribly indefinite," he expostulated.

"What do you mean?"

"Well, in what you're going to seek for."

"I don't know myself what it is, except that I feel
it is there—what I want and need."

Stokes lifted his eyes to the treetops in a vexed

and despairing glance. He felt the uselessness of further attempts to define her purpose.

"It all comes down to that over-worked phrase 'seeing life,'" he stated.

The girl beside him straightened impulsively.

"That's just it—using the words in their best sense," she exclaimed. "Life—people living to the fullest! With all the struggle and strife and pain and joy and swift movement and variety——'"

"And sordidness and degradation and crime and poverty, don't leave them out," Bob put in.

"Yes, if necessary. Those things too."

"I don't believe you know in the least what you're really doing when you plan for that," said he.

"Most assuredly I do."

"I'll continue to retain my doubts."

"You may. But I'm absolutely in earnest; and I know exactly why I'm going and what I want."

Bob looked at the road before him for a time.

"When did you say you were going?" he asked, at length.

"In the autumn."

"Well, I shall have left Martinsport myself long before that time," he said. "Frederic should be up and able to attend to business in six weeks or so, which will enable me to return to Seattle. By the time the first boat is launched, say, or soon after. Think of me once in awhile when you're being jostled about in the metropolis."

And he turned his blue eyes upon her with a quizzical inquiring gaze.

XIX

THE OPENING VISTA

THOUGHT of New York and its anticipated multiplex experiences in store for her suddenly paled and vanished from her mind at his announcement, as the rosy tint of sunset all at once fades from the sky. She felt an odd tremor in her bosom, a sinking of heart, a sense of dismay and bereavement. Martinsport without his presence, his tall active figure and clear eyes and sanguine countenance and cheerful friendly voice, would henceforth be unendurable. She had an instant's fright at the realization of how swiftly and unconsciously he had become the center of her attention, interest, thoughts; of how keen was her enjoyment of his company and how empty the moments when he was absent, of how she waited for his words and thrilled to his vibrant tones, his glance, his very nearness. And she dumbly apprehended that happiness for her was not in any city or multitude for the reasons she had asserted, but would be in whatsoever spot, town or wilderness, he might be. Had he not said—and her breathing almost ceased as her mind encompassed the truth of her feeling—love is not in cities but in the heart?

She ventured a look at his face. It was set straight ahead, a bit thoughtful, a little unhappy even, and decidedly grim. Her plan of going away from Martinsport had distinctly displeased him; and at the recognition of the fact a flutter of joy beat in her breast. He cared whether or not she went away.

"Do you like lumbering better than ship-building?" she asked, after a time.

"I think I should like it as well, if I knew something about it," he replied. "I'm really only managing the general business; Mulhouse is actually the builder. But I'm learning something of how ships are constructed, for I'm absorbing all the knowledge of the craft that I can in a short time. As a matter of fact, I came here chiefly to protect our interests as you know, discover and defeat our enemies, and keep things running as well as possible until Frederic can take hold again."

"Which includes building the ships and launching them," said she, with a smile.

"Yes. That has to be done. Men do things in an emergency many times that they would never dream of doing under ordinary circumstances. Frederic had studied up on the business: he had a fair grasp of it before he began. I had to jump into his place and make up with nerve what I lack in knowledge. He had the audacity the other day to remark——" Stokes broke off, with an amused grin.

"To remark what, if I may ask?"

"That I remain in charge here after he's well,

so that he can give his time to expanding this yard and to starting another in the east somewhere. Shipbuilding's the thing, the big thing of the future, he declares; and he does nothing now while lying in bed but work out plans. A shipyard on the coast at home too is in his mind, where we can use our own lumber. We'll build the ships, he says, and our other brother, John, will finance operations— he's the money-shark of the firm. It sounds well when he's singing the song and has me entranced. But, oh, the gray hairs it would give us all before we were through!"

The girl sat in contemplation for a moment.

"You could run the yard here of course, if you set out to do so," she exclaimed confidently. "Who doubts it! Perhaps you don't know everything about building vessels that's to be known, but I have observed you enough to believe it wouldn't be long before you had a thorough knowledge of the work. You've been studying at the office until long after midnight nights, that is, I suppose you've been studying the matter of ship construction, for one of the guards said you were there. And what a magnificent conception of your brother's for more yards and ships!"

"Well, it's captivating, I admit—if we're not all blown to kindling-wood first," Bob said, with a warmer tone.

"You're not going to be blown up; we'll see to that."

Her determined utterance and vigorous nod, and

the unconscious use of the little word "we," bespeaking comradeship as it did, brought a satisfied smile to Bob's lips and a gleam in his eyes. She was loyal and staunch and courageous. If it were not for that one recalcitrant idea she held of going off to New York——

"I don't believe we shall suffer any harm, with you on hand," said he. "I feel that you bring us luck."

"If I ever bring it, now's the time I ask for it," she stated, giving him a bright look. "I want your company to succeed, and want to see your personal success. Of course I'm employed by your company and that alone is sufficient for my wishing Stokes Brothers to come through with colors flying, but my feeling goes further than that. Until you came I had considerable responsibility keeping the plant running; and brief though it was, that responsibility gave me an interest in the ships as if they were partly my own and that has since continued to grow."

"I understand what you mean," he said, softly.

"Maybe it's the feeling every person has in work with which one has been closely concerned," she went on. "I suppose a violin-maker has it, an engineer who builds a bridge or an irrigation project or a railroad, and every one who really contributes his thought or skill of hands to create something. I see these ships growing in the yard under my very eyes, from piles of rough lumber into huge graceful vessels destined to sail over the seas. Sometimes

I go out and touch them with my hands and caress them. And I really do feel as if I had put something worth while into them, something of myself perhaps, and that it has penetrated the very planks and will remain there and be a part of the ships. If they were blown up, the injury would be a wound to me, it seems. And so that is why I am so anxious for your company's success and your success, because in this way the ships belong to me too; I tell myself I'm one of the builders. Some people might laugh and say I'm too imaginative."

"Those who did would have souls of slugs," Bob Stokes declared quickly.

"It's my reason too why I feel that nothing must happen or can happen to destroy the vessels," she said.

"I repeat, you brought us luck when you set foot in our yard. You were sent as a special dispensation of Providence to overcome the bad 'influence' in the outer office." And Bob's face as he gazed about at her might have been a confirmation of his words.

Ellen laughed softly.

"That makes me see myself in a new light," she said.

"I shall continue to so regard you."

However that might be, he was at the moment regarding her very intently and very earnestly. He would have liked to take one of her small white hands in his and tell her many other things about herself—how her dark glowing eyes were quite won-

derful at that instant, and her cheek and chin possessed of the softest and most exquisite curve im-
aginable, and her hair so thick and rebellious—well,
any number of things which the liking for her had
inspired but which mere friendship did not war-
rant. Like her—why, there wasn't another girl
anywhere who could compare with her! And if
he continued to see much more of her, it would all
be up with him. That was sure; that was certain.
And she would go away to New York, and he would
have only a heartache; he was without doubt about
the heartache, for he had a dull, empty, hungry
longing somewhere in his breast now.

The car had been moving westward as they talked
and came now through thinning pines out on open
ground. Before them shimmered the waters of a
bayou that stretched away into the interior, its bor-
ders grown with thick marsh grass, a faint smell of
mud and salt water coming from its direction, while
on its lazy surface floated an oyster boat. Gulls
flew about, crying and quarreling and settling down
upon the waves.

The road here bent south and Stokes uttered an
exclamation of satisfaction at this fact. It led
towards the gulf, where they would be able to gain
eventually the shell road along the beach and thus
return to Martinsport without retracing the route
the car had come.

"I engage you now for another drive next Sunday, if you have no other plans for then," Bob
spoke. "We toilers ought as a matter of health

come into the fresh air as much as possible. Think
what we endure when the wind is blowing from the
canneries."

His air of badinage only half-masked his expect-
ance.

"Next Sunday is a whole week away; much might
happen in that time," said she.

"Of course. But there's no reason why we
shouldn't make plans just the same. And in the
meanwhile we'll have another boat ride or two;
just when, you will decide. I'm counting on them
also."

The insistence of his manner grew with each
succeeding statement. Ellen perceived that he was
again looking at her, so steadfastly and appealingly
that once more she experienced a tremor of heart
and a sensation of being drawn towards him by invisible cords. An intuitive need to resist seemed for
some reason imperative.

"Let me answer to-morrow or next day," she said,
turning away her eyes.

"But we'll have the boat rides?"

"Yes. Sometime soon."

"Why not to-morrow night if the weather is
clear? If we don't take advantage of good eve-
nings, first thing we know a storm will roll up and
it will be foggy and wet for a fortnight, as I'm told
is frequently the case. Then I'd be just sitting
around gnawing my finger-nails and gazing at you
remorsefully."

Ellen could not forego a smile at the picture he

drew.   But nevertheless her feelings were in a
baffling state of confusion—pleasure, uncertainty,
and fear of where everything appeared to be leading.   Each minute with him was a delight, and if
she but abandoned herself to her desire she would
have given her consent to his invitation immediately, yet a medley of dreads impinged upon her mind.
Formless, for the most part.

"You don't answer me," came his voice, with a
low intonation.

"I was thinking.   I have things to do at home,
and I had best stay there to-morrow evening and
do them."

The car lurched in a hollow of sand.   Stokes
gave the wheel a vicious twist, muttering something
under his breath.   The more persistently she evaded
his wish, the more obstinately determined he became that the girl beside him should see that he was
in earnest.

"One can always do things at home any time.   If
I appear at your house after supper to take you
boating, you wouldn't make a scene to prevent me,
would you?"

Ellen's blood began to flow faster in her veins.
He looked quite as if he were capable of picking
her up in the face of all the boarders and carrying
her away.   Indeed, his blue eyes held a hot blaze
in their depths that blinded her for the instant to
all else.

"I might enjoy being—snatched up," she murmured.

"Then expect me to-morrow evening," said he.

"Really, Mr. Stokes, I have necessary things to do."

He gave a shake of his head.

"You speak seriously, so I'll urge you no further," he said. "But you will go in the motor boat with me—adventuring again, let us say—as soon as convenient?"

Ah, adventuring! Where was her heart drifting in his company? Her lids drooped. The dusky half-veiled light Bob so often had beheld in her eyes now dwelt in them.

"Yes, why not?" she said, softly.

"Why not, of course," he echoed. "Now that is settled."

"Perhaps Tuesday or Wednesday evening," she said.

"And another auto ride next Sunday; I can count on that too, can't I? Who else do we know in Martinsport besides ourselves, and so why shouldn't we enjoy ourselves together?"

A vision of New York as she had pictured it in her fancy, with all she had anticipated and hoped for there, arose in Ellen Durand's mind. She would not in any case go there until autumn, and if Bob Stokes went away from Martinsport in July, or whenever he went if he did go, it would make no difference then how soon she departed. And in the meantime? Then all at once she was conscious that there would be no more of New York, or anything else in her life to bring her happiness but

the youth beside her. The truth smote her sharply
—and it seemed as if a low joy was moving in her
heart. The matter of what she did or where she
went was no longer one of choice. It had somehow
been irrevocably settled. She loved him: the earth
might revolve backward without changing that mo-
mentous fact.

"Yes, I'll go with you next Sunday," she answered, as if she had never discussed the question.
"At the same hour as to-day."

"Good. I'll put a red mark on the date, for it
will be a red-letter day."

She regarded him to see if he had observed the
tremendous thing which had occurred with her, that
by all logic should show like a luminous light on
her face for every one to read. But Bob glanced
at her smilingly and then away at the road ahead,
as if he saw no difference there from what had
been before. Thank heaven, he had seen nothing.
Then her mind was assailed by a sudden dread:
he appeared fond of her—but was she destined to
love without return? What if her love ended in
lone tragedy?

XX

EVIDENCE OF GUILT

A HEAVY fog enveloped sea and land. The hulls
of the vessels in the shipyard appeared huge and
indistinct, while the sounds of labor about them
were deadened by the mist. Water dripped from
the wet wood of scaffolding and ships. A smell
of muggy pine hung in the air.

Bob Stokes gazing out a window of the office,
speculated upon the whereabouts of the two men
who had fled from the island. Had it not been for
Ellen Durand's unfortunate misstep and her involuntary cry which revealed the presence of in-
truders to the pair on the wreck, the conspirators
would now be locked up. As it was, they were
at large with their instruments of destruction. The
police had failed to discover any further track of
them or learn their identity. Unquestionably the
men had gone into hiding, now they suspected their
purpose known, until they were ready to act.

Mulhouse, the superintendent, had reported that
several workmen were under quiet surveillance by
their associates, the principal number of the company's men being enlisted actively in the hunt for
traitors. The sifting out process had thinned the

likely suspects down to six or seven; fellows of rough character. Flanagan was thick with two of these, Mulhouse stated—but all three of them had drawn their pay yesterday noon and quit. The others who were being watched had committed no specific acts of vandalism so far. For that matter, nothing out of the way had occurred in the yard or about the ships since the switch had been spiked.

From Snohomish Jim Bob had received no news, but his action in stopping work and disappearing indicated that he was following some lead. Jim always moved to a purpose and used his own methods. Already a score of workmen had reported him as talking sedition, indeed, as a lawless ruffian by his own account.

Turning from the window Bob gazed at Ellen Durand, who was busy copying a report. Ever since their adventure together on the island, she had had for him a new charm, indefinable, pleasing, born of their intimacy of spirit in the moment of danger. The little upward turn at the corner of her mouth had a sort of enchantment of its own; her glowing eyes seemed but partly to reveal the possibilities, the ardor and the quality of mystery of her nature; even her dusky, rebellious hair possessed a captivating endowment. When he was alone, her face came before him with haunting persistency. And he found himself when she was by unconsciously dwelling on her profile.

As if presently aware of his gaze, she lifted her eyes, meeting his. She passed her hand over the keys of her machine, then withdrew it. Her lashes fluttered slightly. A faint blush suffused her cheeks.

"I'll have the statement finished in a moment," she said, glancing at the paper she copied.

"No hurry. I wasn't thinking of it," Bob replied.

Her look continued on the sheet. Directly she resumed her work, but paused as Bob said:

"When this fog clears we'll try our luck again on the water—perhaps we'll find our Germans a second time. Good fortune seems to follow you."

"But it didn't lead to anything more than that old house and the wreck."

"We learned the men concerned and the nature of their plot," said he. "I wired to the federal authorities at New Orleans what was up and there are government men working with the police on the case. They have a good description of the fellows. It should be only a matter of time before they're apprehended. Now, if you will bring luck once more——" He ceased, smiling.

Ellen Durand shook her head.

"I wish I could," said she.

"Well, we'll have a boat ride when the fog lifts, in any case. I may count on that?"

"Yes, indeed." Then she added, thoughtfully, "I've been wondering, and fearing a little, about the guard in the yard. Something I can't explain makes me sure that the criminals intend to destroy the ships if they're able. It isn't only that ships are the favorite objects of attack by German agents—

there's what has happened before. Blowing the
vessels to pieces now would be just a fitting climax."

Bob nodded.

"Germany desires above everything else to delay
America's output of hulls," he remarked.

Walking to a window he stared out at the nearest
vessel of the two which Stokes Brothers were building. It loomed mighty and staunch in the fog. It
was approaching completion. In a few weeks it
would slide down the way into the waters of the
basin. One more boat to aid in defeating the enemy!
Its building not only involved the firm's interests,
but in a broader degree constituted a unit in the
nation's welfare. Boats the country needed, and
boats the country should have—from Stokes Brothers, at any rate. Enemy plots and bombs, notwithstanding!

"I think there's something I should tell you;
there's too much at stake not to do so," Ellen Durand said, arousing him from his abstraction.

He faced about and came towards her. Her look
was fixed upon him steadily, though her face was
troubled.

"What is that?" he asked.

Again as on the first day he had spoken with her,
her glance sought the closed door to the outer office.

"I find it difficult to speak of the matter," said
she, "for it concerns Mr. Andrews, who has been
kind to me. It seems like the basest sort of ingrati-
tude after he helped me secure this position when

I had newly come to Martinsport and when he's always been obliging and helpful. But at the same time I'd never forgive myself if anything terrible happened through my withholding information."

At her words Bob Stokes glared at the door.

"I suspected that fellow the first time I laid eyes on him," he declared, "and I've suspected him ever since. Now I know he's mixed up in this fight on us. Been the bribed 'lookout' here for the principals. It was he, of course, who went through our files in this room." For a minute he appeared about to burst through the door and immediately pounce on Andrews, then he inquired, "What have you learned of him?"

"Several things," Ellen Durand answered. "First, I just thought him dishonest when I happened to step to the door there one afternoon before you arrived and saw him going through Mr. Mocket's coat pockets on the sly. Mr. Mocket's back was toward him, and at the same time that Mr. Andrews was searching he watched the book-keeper over his shoulder. He was at the coat not more than an instant—and he didn't perceive me."

"Go on," Bob encouraged.

"I don't think he found anything; at least his hands came out empty. After that I began to watch him quietly, as much as I could while attending to work, for I felt that if he were really a thief he should not be employed here, especially when Mr. Frederic Stokes was sick and absent. But I didn't connect him with the accidents in the shipyard

until one noon—just the day before you arrived—
I knew Mr. Mocket had stepped out and so I stole
to the door to see what Mr. Andrews might be
doing. He was busy running a finger down a list
of workmen, muttering to himself. Presently he
said loud enough for me to hear: 'That big-nosed
tough Frenchman would cut a throat for ten dollars, I bet . . . do a job here to delay things . . .
look him up.' That was the manner in which he
spoke; I didn't catch all."

"You heard enough to show where he stands,"
Bob stated, in a significant tone.

"Finally, I made him out talking at the telephone
only yesterday," she continued. "You and Mr.
Mocket were in the warehouse at the time."

"Yes, we were in there, I remember."

"Well, I listened by the door again. Mr. Andrews was talking with some one he called Jim—
he used the name twice. He said, 'Haven't learned
the time yet? Well, there'll be big doings in the
yard when the fireworks start.' He was talking in
a low voice, but the office was quiet and I caught
the words: 'We'll see whether or not Stokes Brothers have a crimp put in their ships. Meantime we
got to get next to the "big man," if we can. And
after the party comes off, a big feed, eh, Jim?' Then
he chuckled and hung up the receiver. See, I took
down his words in shorthand."

"That convicts him, his statement about our ships.
And the scoundrel is in the pay of those German
agents!" Bob said, between his teeth. " 'Fireworks'

means but one thing—bombs! Fortunately no definite time has yet been set for the attempt, judging from what he said. Provision can be made to protect the yard."

"But it seems incredible of Mr. Andrews. I knew his words concerned the vessels, but I can't believe it yet, Mr. Stokes, even though he is dishonest."

"I'll have him arrested to-night. The police will sweat the truth out of him and perhaps too the whereabouts of his accomplices."

"And still I feel unhappy over it," Ellen Durand said, "for it was he who helped me in the beginning when I was looking about for a place. Even if he's bad, it does appear as if I were returning evil for good in informing about him."

"The feeling does you credit," said he, "but you've chosen the right course. You may be sure I'm more than grateful. Your discovery has put one of the criminals in our hands and should lead to the capture of the rest. And in all probability it has aided in saving our ships." He caught and pressed her fingers. "I don't know how to express my sense of obligation, for the company and for myself. I don't know what I should have done without you. I'll not try to express my feeling by mere thanks—but I intend to prove it in a hundred ways."

She trembled under the pressure of his hand, then softly drew her fingers free.

"I'm happy if I helped you the smallest bit," she responded with an uncertain smile.

"Yours is the biggest bit of anybody's."

She risked a look up into his eyes. They were bent so earnestly upon her face that her blood quickened its beat in her bosom. The light of them set her heart in a tumult.

"I must finish my work; it's growing late," she said hastily, and turned and went to her desk.

Bob looked at his watch. The hands showed a few minutes past five. He had an appointment with two gentlemen, Willard and Broussard, who were coming to the office. They were to have arrived and were already late, but he did not know but what he would rather not have them come at all to-day. Mr. Willard had telephoned they wished to see him, which at the time aroused Bob's curiosity. Ever since he had discovered Broussard's connection with Gaudreault he had been mystified about Broussard and the illusive lawsuit which had never come to a head.

He again took a place at the window, gazing out at the long dark body of the visible ship, its farther end buried in the fog. Then he began watching the globules of water course down the window-pane. A steady hum came from the typewriter under Ellen Durand's fingers.

"What the deuce you want to go to New York for is beyond me!" he exclaimed suddenly, with entire irrelevance.

The typewriter stopped. Then the girl said:

"Did you speak, Mr. Stokes?"

He laughed.

"I was merely thinking with my voice," he stated.

"Oh, I see. Well, I'm going to New York because I fear Martinsport will be dull after the excitement has ended here."

Bob gazed at her from under his brows.

"I'll start some of my own, then. You'll be too busy to go."

Ellen Durand was saved the need of an answer by the opening of the door. Mr. Mocket ushered the expected visitors into the room.

"These gentlemen to see you," he stated, stepping aside to allow the men to enter.

He waited for them to pass, standing erect and passive. As Broussard sauntered in, he gave the book-keeper a long and somewhat insolent look, which the other appeared not to perceive. At a nod from Stokes, Ellen Durand slipped out of her seat and withdrew from the room. Her also Broussard observed with a flicker of interest. Finally when Mocket had gone out, he turned his scrutiny upon Bob Stokes, running his eyes over the young fellow's figure and face with a slow, contemplative air. Broussard had the free assurance, Bob judged, of a man not easily abashed.

XXI

AN UNEXPECTED ALLY

"WE shall not detain you long, Mr. Stokes," Broussard said after he had been introduced to Bob and when the three men were seated. "I've been in conference with Mr. Willard relative to certain matters of interest to you, particularly in regard to the attack made on your brother and those on your property."

Bob Stokes somewhat puzzled as to the visitor's concern in the matter looked towards Mr. Willard.

That gentleman had lighted one of his thin, black, rakish-appearing cigars according to his custom when beginning a discussion. He nodded in confirmation.

"Mr. Broussard has acquired the note and collateral stock held by Johnson and Farrington," he said. "We were correct in surmising that there was a move on foot to throttle and obtain if possible control of your business. In the beginning, a number of men, including Mr. Broussard, sought to buy stock of your brother with a view of later freezing your company out."

"Don't include me in that part; I wasn't so simple," Broussard interrupted.

"Well, the others had conceived such a scheme at any rate. But when it was learned no stock was for sale," Willard went on, "Johnson and Farrington apparently hoped to use this loan to accomplish the same end for themselves. Now, Mr. Broussard."

With a sardonic smile Broussard removed his cigarette in order to speak. He flipped the ash off its end with a delicate finger.

"The thing is really amusing, especially the manner in which I trimmed Johnson and old Farrington out of twenty-five thousand and the note's interest," he said, "while they imagined they were handing me a gold brick. You have had the joy of their acquaintance, I take it, Mr. Stokes. They had excluded me from any raid on your company," he proceeded unblushingly, "or I should never have meddled. Besides, that pair of foxes must have their ears nicked about every so often. They didn't know I was aware they had made the loan, but Main dropped word of it one day. So I prepared a lawsuit——"

"I know about it—that fellow Gaudreault," said Bob.

"Eh? Why, this is interesting. But no matter; it was a fake designed to scare the bankers. Your mortgage coming just when it did helped immensely. They shook the paper out of their clothes and I walked off with it. But they spoke of attacks on your property by some one unknown, so I began to investigate on my own account now that I held some of your paper. And I looked first among thieves of my acquaintance."

Again the smile shaped his lips, while his eyes rested amusedly on Stokes. The latter, on his part, knew not what to make of the singular recital, or of the gentleman himself who talked rather indolently of his business as if engaged in nothing but lawless enterprises. Broussard, he was aware, was one of the town's leading capitalists, but he might by his talk have been anything else.

"Yes," Bob said, tentatively.

"Johnson and Farrington being eliminated, I turned to the next likely quarter, two men of the name of Main and Derland, both highly respected citizens and capable freebooters. Derland, I quickly learned, was not in the least concerned in the deal. But Main was in the running. His information to me in the beginning that the bankers had made the loan, which I suspect he had from this office——"

"This office!" Bob ejaculated.

"No doubt of it—but let that go for the present. Which he had from this office, and his accompanying threat that he would get their goat, as he had told them if he were left out, gave me a lead. When did your troubles begin, Mr. Stokes?"

"Shortly after the loan was made."

"Well, I imagined so. Or soon after Main knew of the loan, we'll say. The other evening I had him to dinner to talk over some matters of business and saw that he partook of a very old, heady wine. He did not know I held your paper. And

when I introduced the subject of Johnson and Farrington holding out on the rest of us, he talked
rather more than he would have done had he been
entirely sober. At that he had loaded several high-
balls into his system at the club before coming. I
obtained no specific details, but he made enough
boasts about killing the loan and getting it himself
at a bargain to satisfy me he had inside knowledge
of conditions and their cause in your business."

"Did he plan my brother's injury?" Bob asked
fiercely, leaning forward.

"Oh, I imagine not. He wouldn't bother with details, he wouldn't want to know them, in fact; that
would be left to his lieutenant. He would say, for
instance, I want work on those ships delayed. That
would be enough; his hands would be clean; he
could rightly deny any knowledge of what had occurred. Isn't that the customary procedure, Mr.
Willard?"

Willard smiled. One might have supposed Broussard was discussing a matter of mere business practice.

"He's guilty nevertheless," Bob asserted, darkly.

"Proving it in court is generally difficult, however, particularly when his handy man vanishes, as
would probably happen, on a journey to the tropics."

Bob looked first at one and then the other of his
visitors.

"Surely there's some way of landing a scoundrel
like that," he stated. "We ought to catch him on the
bomb part of it, anyway. Any man who would at

this time when our country's at war deliberately encourage the blowing up of ships ought to be hanged."

Willard suddenly hitched himself up in his chair to gaze at Stokes. Broussard halted the hand that was lifting his cigarette to his lips.

"What's that about bombs?" he demanded, all alertness.

"Bombs are what I'm talking about. I ran on two men the other night who were manufacturing them to blow up our works. A clerk in our office——"

"Yes, the fellow used to be Main's private clerk," Broussard broke in, with a nod.

"This clerk was overheard telephoning only yesterday to a confederate about the execution of the plot. When I discovered the men with the explosives I notified the police, but the scoundrels had taken alarm and escaped. Federal officers also are now on the case."

"Well, well, well. That surprises me; I've underrated Main, I see," Broussard exclaimed.

"I'll make it my especial business to see he goes to prison if this prove true," Willard announced, with a sharp glint in his blue eyes. "But I'll send him there anyway for injuring Stokes."

For a moment Broussard reflected, a line of smoke rising from the cigarette between his fingers. His smile was gone.

"Mr. Stokes, let me first state, speaking seriously, that while I offered to buy stock in your company of your brother," he said, "it was purely because

I considered the investment a good one and when he declined to sell I considered that the end of the matter. At least, at the time. I looked upon your coming here as a valuable asset to Martinsport; I had no feeling other than of good wishes for your success in your enterprise. A man who snarls at another's good luck, or rather wise foresight, is both a fool and a glutton. And when finally I entered the game it was merely to take a fall out of Johnson and Farrington. I didn't care particularly to buy your paper, but on the other hand I knew it was perfectly good. You can take it up any time you desire, or I'll extend it at your pleasure. In any case, the note is better in my hands than in those of the men who made the loan and who had some scheme, I feel confident, to squeeze you. I didn't want to see those money-sharks crimp a legitimate and valuable business for no other reason than their own selfish gain."

"Thank you, Mr. Broussard. I appreciate your consideration," Bob stated. "We were not aware that we had in you an unknown and disinterested friend."

"My interest was there—but it was focused on Farrington primarily," came the response, with a quick sharp show of teeth in a smile. "With Johnson and Farrington disposed of and learning that Main was in for mischief, I considered some means of putting him out of the ring also. But I had not yet decided upon a plan—I thought it best first to talk with Mr. Willard, who holds your mortgage,

and with you. That is my explanation for being
here. Now, your revelation regarding a deliberate
attempt at destruction of the property throws a new
and serious light on the matter. Well as I knew
'Gas' Main, I didn't imagine he would go to the
length he apparently proposes to do. He's a good
deal of a brute, however. If anything stands in his
way, smash it—that's his method. If it's a man,
smash him. And he cares little if bystanders are
hurt in the process. He was trying to revenge himself on Johnson and Farrington for what he thought
their trickery towards him when he instigated secret obstructive tactics against your concern. If by
delays and accidents he could depreciate their loan,
why, the fact you might be bankrupted in the process wouldn't disturb him. He had it calculated
that with a failure to complete your ships on time,
you would collapse and the pair of bankers conse-
quently suffer, while incidentally he might step in
and pick up your property at a forced sale. Very
likely that was his idea. Very likely he determined
to make the matter certain." Broussard shook his
head in perplexity. "But it doesn't seem after all
he could be so mad as to blow up your yard. The
man is shrewd for all his brutal nature. I confess
that I'm mystified."

"Listen, I even saw the bombs. And the clerk
here discussed the planned outrage with some one
over the telephone, as I stated," Bob said.

"It's time 'Gas' Main went where his activities

will be restricted," Mr. Willard asserted. "Count on me to fight this thing to a finish now."

"He'll feel satisfied with the new clothes he'll have, at any rate," Broussard remarked, smiling. "He's always had a predilection for loud stripes."

Bob considered for a little.

"We were ready for any financial operations of our enemies," he remarked. "My brother in Seattle, John, had arrangements made to turn the property over to the government, by lease or otherwise, the instant Johnson and Farrington or any one else sought to get control, which would leave them in the air so far as making a killing was concerned. We would have sat back and watched the government make them behave—and they would have been glad to let go. The iron would be too hot. As it is, we plan when these ships are sold to build for the Ship Board at only a nominal profit. This is no time, we feel, even if our yard should not be commandeered, to let big war-time profits influence us against the country's interests. We desire to sell these two vessels privately only in order to put the business in good shape against emergencies, then we'll be ready to construct boats for government use at cost if necessary."

"Now I really am sorry I don't own stock," Broussard said, spreading his hands in a gesture of pleasure. "For I too, though the devil himself deny it, have an interest in America's success in this war. All I've been able to do up to date is subscribe for Liberty Bonds and the Red Cross Fund and so on. That's rather passive. Presently Willard and I may furnish an ambulance outfit, though Willard doesn't know it—the idea has just occurred to me. A string of forty ambulances, say, with a whole company of pretty nurses! But let that wait. We're now dealing with the subject of Main. It looks very much as if we'd have to put him behind bars—I'd rather miss his bull manner at directors' meetings, too. Still, Farrington might grow more amusing as time passed. Gentlemen, I am for punishing," he continued, with a sudden rap of his knuckles on the table, "punishing any man, big or little, wealthy or poor, American or alien, who at this time commits an act that is an injury, directly or indirectly, to our country. He is disloyal and an enemy. And 'Gas' Main apparently is such a man."

"But can we have him arrested now?" Bob questioned.

"No, not till the evidence is complete," Broussard answered.

"What of this clerk?" Willard asked.

"We could have him in here," Bob said.

But Broussard raised a dissenting hand.

"It might be well before interrogating the man— Mocket is his name, if I remember rightly——"

Stokes gave a start.

"Why, Mocket has nothing to do with the matter," he exclaimed. "The fellow I've referred to is named Andrews."

Striking a match and lighting a fresh cigarette Broussard inhaled a slow puff before replying. He swung about in his chair and gazed fixedly at the door.

"The man who was Main's private clerk and who is now out there is the tall, spare fellow wearing glasses. No mistake. I had a good look at him as I entered," he said. "I've seen him dozens of times in Main's offices formerly. He handled that piece of strike business for Main last summer, though he didn't appear in it prominently. I know nothing about this Andrews you speak of. But you'll find that the information of your loan, and probably of other matters, went straight from here into Main's office from this Mocket."

"He's been with us ever since the yard was started," Bob said, in perplexity.

"Well, I can't account for that, but Mocket was 'Gas' Main's private clerk for some time. The thing is quite clear now. He's Main's man and has handled this office end of the little private war. There's your trouble-maker, Mr. Stokes, I'll venture my head."

Willard, who had remained silent, occasionally puffing at his cigar and stroking his white silky beard, now spoke.

"We must proceed with care, until we gather proof of Main's complicity," said he. "That requires time. Meanwhile means must be taken to protect the property and prevent or delay the effort at its attempted destruction. What would hold his hand, Broussard? A belief he had bested Johnson and Farrington?"

"Unquestionably."

"Then this note and its security must go into his possession. You might intimate——"

Broussard sprang up.

"Leave it to me. If you'll allow me to use that 'phone, Stokes, I'll see if I can get in touch with him. I'll try his private number—he may yet be at his office."

He seated himself in the chair which Bob relinquished at the desk and put in the call.

"Hello, this you, Main? Thought I might catch you there. You remember what you were speaking of the other evening at my house. . . . Yes, that loan. Well, I picked it up. . . . Certainly you can have it. They appeared to have had enough, but wanted to sell to me instead of you. . . . Sore as anything that they had to let go. . . . Ha, you're right. To anybody but you! They'd probably go up in the air if they thought I'd passed it along. I'll be up to see you immediately. . . . One seventy-five. You can have it for what I paid. Farrington would rather have parted with his ears than lose that twenty-five. . . . All right, you wait. It's barely six o'clock. I'll start at once."

Broussard hung up the receiver. Then he drew an envelope from his pocket, removed several papers which he ran over rapidly.

"You've the note and stock with you, I see," Bob said.

"Yes, I brought them along in case you should

want them to use or desired to make a new note for a longer period."

"And at one time I suspected you of being the main plotter!" Bob exclaimed, putting out his hand to the other.

Broussard shook the hand offered. He then resumed his indolent air. He twisted the end of his Vandyke, while his brilliant black eyes roved round the room.

"I've a sinister reputation with Johnson and Farrington, at least," said he. "For one thing, I don't press loans—that's a black sin. For another, I'm a bachelor; they imagine me decidedly wicked. Well, Mr. Willard, if you'll drop me out at the door of Main's building, I'll be taking my departure. Possibly I'll be able to gain an inkling from Main what effect his securing the paper will have on his plans."

Stokes again expressed his thanks for the service both of the gentlemen had rendered in interesting themselves in the company's behalf and they went out. A moment later Willard's car sounded from in front of the building. Bob stepped into the outer office, where Ellen Durand stood looking out the door at the machine which was starting away.

"I'm sorry to have kept you out of the room so long," he said, "but we were engaged in an important talk. You've been delayed in going home; it's after six. But I'll run you up there in my car. The men have gone, I see."

"They both left about half-past five, first Mr.

Mocket and then a moment later Mr. Andrews," she answered.

"That's rather unusual; I might have wanted them."

"They've both absented themselves from the office a good deal lately during business hours. Often at the same time," she said.

"Well, I'll soon know why," he remarked significantly.

"I asked Mr. Mocket if he'd be back and he answered 'No' very shortly," she continued.

"Did Andrews have anything to say?"

"Nothing. When Mr. Mocket left, the other fidgeted a little, went to the door and looked out, then suddenly got his coat and hat and started away too. He looked at me as if he dared me to say a word. But I remained quiet; he knows quite as well as I do that he is supposed to stay until six."

After a glance Bob moved forward and passed behind the counter.

"The books haven't even been put away," he exclaimed.

On the men's desks the company ledgers and papers remained as they had been left. Bob pushed the latter into drawers, carried the books to the safe and placed them within. He opened a small compartment and glanced in its box in precaution before swinging shut the heavy iron door.

"There's usually some cash here, isn't there?" he inquired.

"Why, I think so. We need a little from time to

time and generally keep an amount on hand—any-where from fifty to one hundred dollars."

Bob closed the door of the safe and spun the knob. Then he once more came out from behind the counter.

"Well, there's none there now," said he.

"That's funny; there's always a little. Wasn't there a single penny?"

"Not one. However, there's going to be a house-cleaning soon. We'll know a bit more then than we do now. Find your hat while I'm bringing the car around. We'll lock up and start. One thing certain, I haven't lost you yet."

XXII

THE MASK OFF

ANDREWS, trailing the book-keeper along the foggy street, had cast all thought of office responsibility to the four quarters of the earth and was bent only on keeping the man's figure in sight. A reprimand for quitting his work gave him no concern; he felt in Mocket's sudden departure an important move in the game that was being played. He had heard nothing from Jim Flanagan, but circumstances might have arisen to prevent the latter from conveying any information to him, if indeed he had it. The book-keeper, however, had emptied the cash drawer of the safe—Andrews, while talking with Ellen Durand, had observed him at the business. The man's action had been furtive. Then Mocket had taken his hat and gone. That looked as if the fellow was cleaning up things before flight.

On the main street of the business section Mocket swung upon a street car. In chagrin the young fellow watched him vanishing, but next minute running to a taxicab awaiting by the curb, he sprang up beside the chauffeur and ordered him to follow the car. The chase led to Mocket's boarding-house. Andrews, sitting in the automobile at the corner beyond, kept the house under observation. Time passed; he saw by his watch that it was after six; he felt the coins in his pocket and anxiously calculated the rate of the taxi charge. At a quarter past six Mocket again appeared, now carrying a suitcase. This time he took a street car returning to the city, alighted near a tall business block and entered a corner cigar shop. Andrews paid his chauffeur and dismissed the cab.

From the vantage of the now crowded street, busy with the homeward bound throng, the young fellow perceived through the open doorway that Mocket was making a purchase of a box of cigars. This together with his suitcase he left in the place. Coming forth, the book-keeper went along the street until he arrived at the doorway of a lofty office building —the building where Main and his gas company had offices. Andrews knew the structure very well.

He loitered a sufficient length of time to allow the other to ascend to the suite, then followed. The building was already emptied of its day-time multitude; a single elevator was running; the hallways were silent; doors wore an air of business having been finished. Stepping forth on the floor above that where Main officed, the fourth, he descended the stair and went noiselessly along the doorways that marked the suite. From one room came a barely audible sound of voices; at the door of another, standing ajar, he caught a glimpse of the interior and of Mocket, who stood with his back towards him listening by a doorway connecting with the room where ran the voices. It was apparent the book-keeper had let himself in with a key he carried without disturbing the occupants. Except for the talkers, Mocket and himself, no one was about. The floor was deserted.

All at once Andrews glided to a doorway beyond and there flattened himself against the panel. A man had come forth from the room where the conversation had been conducted—Broussard. He walked towards the elevator and presently was carried down. Silence again prevailed after the echoes of his footsteps ceased; only diminished noises ascended from the street.

Once more the youth crept to his post. Mocket was no longer visible, but the connecting door of the rooms was partly open and a new exchange of talk was proceeding. Andrews could even distinguish the respective tones of the men, though unable to hear clearly their words. One was the voice of Mocket, the other he presumed to be Main's. For some minutes he listened, but with a growing annoyance at not being able to overhear the subject of their speech. Finally with a quick glance in all directions he insinuated his body through the narrow opening.

* * * * * * *

The door had scarcely closed behind Broussard when Mocket entered where Main still sat, the note and collateral which he had received in exchange for a check still in his fingers. The gas magnate eyed this new and unannounced visitor with a heavy questioning stare.

"Where in the devil did you come from!" he demanded.

"I just arrived, Mr. Main," was the answer. "Observing that you were occupied and finding the door of the room yonder unlocked, I stepped in to wait until you had finished. I came on the chance that you might yet be here, wishing to report."

"Well?"

"Matters are advancing in accordance with your desire. There will be new developments presently that will put a stop to Stokes Brothers' business for some time."

The man still stood. He spoke in an even tone and when he ceased addressing Main remained with his thin lips compressed in a hard inflexible line. The other drummed upon the table with the fingers of one hand, contemplating him. His big bulk filled the chair in which he sat; the flesh of his cheeks and neck bore down his collar; his thick nose and traplike mouth more than ever gave him an aspect of ruthlessness.

"You can stop further operations for the time," said he, shortly.

"Haven't results been satisfactory?" Mocket inquired. "From the first delay to the accident that removed Stokes——"

"Stop! I've told you I do not want to know what was done, only that things were done," Main exclaimed. "And now you will let matters rest where they are. I've accomplished what I sought—secured this note that Johnson and Farrington held. That's all I wanted."

"Very well, sir. I'll pay the men something so they'll be satisfied and call them off. You had better give me the money now."

"How much will you need?" Main asked.

"A couple of hundred dollars," Mocket stated.

Main looked at him stonily for a moment, but his lieutenant's face continued calm.

"You don't believe in economy, do you?" he said with a sneer.

"Men employed as these have been make high terms," the book-keeper answered. "I've had a little less than a thousand dollars, in addition to what you've paid me myself. You've obtained Stokes Brothers' note, no doubt considerably below the face. The investment has been a good one, hasn't it, Mr. Main?"

"I'll lose nothing, I think."

"So I believe," Mocket went on. "We had no specific agreement at the time of our arrangement as to what I should receive, but you intimated that if the work was carried through successfully I could count on your generosity."

"You've had five hundred for yourself."

"I think I'm entitled to at least that much more," Mocket remarked, quietly.

"Well, you'll not get it."

And "Gas" Main settled himself in his seat and began cutting the end of a cigar with his cigar-clipper. He did not even glance up at Mocket during the operation. A cold smile rested on the lips of the man whom he chose to ignore, while his eyes narrowed behind their glasses.

"At least you will pay what's owing the men," said the latter, presently.

"I think you've pocketed half of what you pretend has gone into expenses, but I'll pay you this two hundred," Main said.

He lighted his cigar and laid the note and the stock certificate on his desk, placing a paper weight upon them. Then he arose. Taking a step to his private safe nearby the desk, he swung the door open; behind him Mocket lightly bent forward, extracted the note and stock from under the weight and advanced soundlessly to where Main stood. The latter was drawing forth a drawer. He straightened and placed it upon the top of the safe.

"Don't trouble to count it," Mocket said, at his ear.

Main whirled about. His secret employee pointed a revolver at his fancy waistcoat. With his left hand the book-keeper removed several packets of bills that half-filled the drawer.

"You thief, there's over two thousand there! I'll have you in the pen for this!" Main said.

"I think not—I know too much. Now sit down in your chair while I talk a little," Mocket ordered. "If you try to attack me, I'll shoot."

Stepping back, he motioned his late employer but

now immediate victim into his seat. Main, breathing heavily, sat down.

"You'll go to the pen, no matter how much you know or talk," he hissed, glaring from under his brows.

"I'm leaving town this evening, so I imagine you'll find some difficulty in carrying out your threat. For your information I'll state that this isn't all of your contribution," Mocket continued, in a voice of irony. "I've cashed a few checks bearing your name, in the course of the day. And you may be interested in knowing that the money will be used in a worthy cause."

"Well?"

"As will be the money secured when I've hypothecated the note and stock in my pocket."

Main glanced swiftly at his desk, perceived the papers missing and half-rose to lunge at the man who had stolen them. But at the forward thrust of the pistol and the menace in Mocket's face, he sank back in his chair, his fingers working helplessly on its arms.

"Play out your string—it won't be for long," he said. And with a sudden calmness he picked up his cigar from the table and began to smoke, keeping his eyes steadfastly upon his assailant.

"That will be seen. But you'll go far to get me!" was the response, given with a new and unexpected violence. "I'm departing from this cursed country and collecting what's coming to me and paying my scores before I go. You thought I'd do your dirty work, then slink out of sight at a word. Last summer after I had managed your band of strike-breaking thugs you discharged me on an unproved complaint of embezzlement of a miserable three hundred dollars. But you came to me for your dirty job at Stokes' yard just the same. Well, I did embezzle the three hundred. Last fall I accepted your commission to hurt the shipping company too, because I was after you and them and anybody else I could harm. For it would help Germany just that much!"

"Germany!" escaped Main's lips, who was astonished in spite of himself.

"Yes, Germany—the Fatherland!" the man cried, with a fire of fanaticism in his eyes. "The country I belong to, the nation destined to rule the world and crush all peoples beneath her iron heel till they recognize her power and right! America, faugh! It will be humbled with the rest. You thought me an American, and well I concealed my nationality." He drew his thin spare figure into an attitude of stiffness. "I'm a German kept here by the war and unable to give my services to my Emperor—I'm none of your American rabble. And when you thought you were simply hiring me to do your scurvy tricks, I was taking your money and laughing at you in my sleeve for the fat swine you are."

"Well?" Main asked again, with implacable patience.

"You imagine you'll run me down. Very well, try it—my provisions are made. I shall tie you up here and gag you however, until I've had plenty of time to go. There'll be time too before you're released to plan my capture."

From his pocket the erstwhile book-keeper brought forth a gag and ball of heavy cord, which he placed on the table.

"You'll be taken and hung before you ever reach Germany," Main stated. "I'll bide my time, Mocket."

"Mocket—Mocket, a name I relinquish here and now! It has served its use. You'll go searching for a Mocket and never find him. And so will the Stokes, and the police, and all the crew of government agents who are so stupid their eyes are never open, when I'm done. You said for me to stop operations. Ah, I've just begun with the shipyard! Those ships will never carry grain to Germany's infamous enemies! The bombs that shall blow them to bits——"

"You've used my scheme as a cover for destroying Stokes' vessels, is that it?" Main asked in a soft voice.

But his body had grown taut, his feet were a little shifted to a new position.

"Just that. Not a stick will be left of them when I'm done to-night. To that extent I'll work for the Fatherland!"

"And you're a German?"

A sharp smile was on Main's lips. He leaned forward in his seat and looked up at the other with a queer strained look on his face.

"A German."

"By God, you'll never live to harm America!"
burst furiously from "Gas" Main's lips, while at
the same time he hurled himself at the alien.

His hands clutched the other's arms. His dis-
torted features pressed towards the book-keeper's.
The suddenness of his attack bent the man back on
the table, who with a desperate exertion shoved
his weapon against Main's body and pulled the
trigger.

For an instant they remained as they were, at
grips. Then the huge capitalist's fingers relaxed,
his eyes blinked rapidly, and he sank down on his
knees.

"You scoundrel!" he muttered.

Then he fell forward on his face under the table.

At that minute the man who had fired the shot
was aware of a figure springing at him through the
inner door. He whirled about as Andrews dashed
forward with face ablaze. The pistol flashed a second time. Andrews halted with a queer look. All
at once he tumbled over.

Through the room the sound of the shots still
echoed. But when silence followed, a hush now all
the more profound, the man who had called himself
Mocket put away his revolver, glanced at his vic-
tims and stood hearkening for an alarm. None
came. The rigidity of his listening attitude slowly
passed. He went to the door and saw that it was
properly locked. He moved with quick, alert steps
and with a frowning intentness on his thin austere
face. In the second room, where half an hour

earlier he had made his treacherous entry, he heark-
ened again. The building gave no sound of voices
or of hurrying footsteps. All was hushed, and only
the acrid smell of powder smoke drifted through
the offices. It caused him to look back where the
two forms lay. He consulted his watch—a quarter
past seven. Presently he went out into the hallway,
listening to make sure that the lock clicked behind
him.

XXIII

SNOHOMISH JIM CLEARS FOR ACTION

In a cheap workingmen's hotel Jim Flanagan and his companions, Pete and Jack, sat together in a retired corner holding aloof from other laborers, who, done their day's work, read tattered magazines or engaged in idle talk. The clock had for Pete and Jack an uncommon attraction; they continually stole looks at it suspended on the wall over the proprietor's small desk—the hands were creeping near the hour of eight. The two men talked little and sat smoking with a light of suppressed excitement in their eyes, hardly heeding Jim's loquacious remarks on the weather.

"They wouldn't call this no fog in Seattle, where I was once. There's what you might call a regular bull fog out there, boys," he was saying. "Here it is going on eight and the nigger just turning on the lights, but when one of them fogs settles down on Seattle the lights are burning all the time and even then a feller has to get close up to 'em to see whether he still is wearing any clothes below his belt."

"Um-m-m," Jack emitted, with an absent air.

"Fact," Snohomish Jim declared, positively. "I was sitting in a hotel once, like this, and when I got up to walk I felt something holding to my pants leg and moving along with me. Well, boys, I lighted a match and went down exploring and what does I behold but a pair of twins, little babies just able to walk, the innocentest little devils you ever see!"

"Huh."

"They had let go their pa sitting next to me, though I didn't know he was by my side, and took a grip on me through an error of judgment like. And it was maybe an hour before I locates their parent in the fog and delivers his progeny, them getting hungry and yelping for maternal milk. Hello, here we are!"

For all his apparent inattention, Snohomish Jim was the first to see the messenger boy entering the office door. A brief telephone message to Pete earlier in the day had advised the trio to be ready that night and to expect money and instructions at eight, as arranged. Jim sprang up and met the boy near the door.

"Here you are," said he, taking the package from the messenger's fingers. "Where's the receipt?"

He scribbled Pete Brown's name on the sheet presented before Pete could forestall him, and turned towards the hallway where the stair led up to their bedrooms, motioning his companions to follow.

"What you got to do with taking that?" Pete demanded viciously, when Jim had locked the door of his room which they had entered.

The speaker glared at the package in the other's hand as if about to grab it away.

"Let's see what we're to do now," Jim said, ignoring the question.

Ripping the long envelope open with a finger, he removed an inner package, from which he slipped off the wrapping. A letter and a mass of currency came to view.

"There's the cash all right!" Jack exclaimed, avidly.

Jim opened the letter.

"Says to be at the northeast corner of the yard fence in half an hour, boys," said he, after rapidly glancing over the message on the sheet. "And each to come alone not to attract notice. That's all. We've time for a drink first."

Still clutching the letter and money in one hand, he produced a quart bottle of whiskey from the bottom of the washstand and handed it to Jack. The latter gulped down an ample quantity and passed it to Pete, who did likewise. Jim in his turn gave it a tilt.

"Well, we'll start," said he, placing the bottle on a chair. "I'll be banker till we're through with the job, when we can divide." And he stuffed the bills and letter into a hip pocket.

Pete and Jack leaped in front of him with snarls.

"You don't work that racket; we split now!" Jack cried, with an oath. "We'd never see you again!"

"Why, pals, what's the matter?" Jim inquired, mildly.

He regarded them with cool insolence, rubbing

the end of his big crooked nose with his forefinger. Pete and Jim exchanged a swift, furtive look.

"Put that money on the table so we can split it," said Pete.

"You're two to one—I'd be done out of my share," Jim answered. "When we're finished at the yard, we'll sit down in a corner and divide it all comfortable and easy. I'm taking no chances."

Again the quick look passed between Pete and Jack. Then the latter began to sidle around one side of Flanagan. Venom was in the sooty faces of both men and a steely gleam in their narrowed eyes.

"Come across with it!" Pete spat out.

"Pals, I has a duty to myself," Jim remarked with a solemn gesture of his big hand.

"Come across, I said!"

Snohomish Jim with a sudden thrust protruded his jaw. His mouth was more askew than ever and shut tight. His whole hard ugly countenance showed sneering defiance.

"Come and get it," he said, barely moving his lips.

For the length of a breath the men remained rigid, while the silence of the dingy bedroom was unbroken. Then at the same instant Pete and Jack rushed him.

Bedlam broke loose. The two men were powerful, hard-muscled, tough, while inspired by baffled greed and a desire for revenge. Snohomish Jim towered three inches over both, with thews and bone wrought by years of swinging an ax and of

driving logs into a frame of iron. All the tricks of
rough-and-tumble fighting, born of the lumber- and
logging-camps, were his. And the time had come at
last to settle the score of Frederic Stokes' cowardly
disablement. The three entwined bodies rocked for
a moment, then went crashing to the floor, rolling
over and over in fury.

The chair and the bottle of whiskey went spinning
across the room. At a quick jab of Jim's knee upward, Jack emitted a grunt of pain, but yet clung
to the woodsman. Jim sank his teeth in Pete's
shoulder in a savage bite, which brought forth a
blood-curdling yell and a panted string of wild
curses. Up by a tremendous heave the three came
to their feet; a struggling, writhing mass they
swayed and thrashed about the room. The bed col-
lapsed as they toppled over on it, but they continued
to strike and fight in its wreck, rolling forth in a
welter of bed-clothes to jolt against the washstand,
which went over with a smash of its pitcher and
bowl.

Blood smeared Jack's face. A mad grin displayed Jim's teeth at the sight. Once more there
was an upheaval and the three men were on their
feet, fighting in silence. By a quick, powerful exertion Snohomish Jim ripped himself out of Pete's
grip, and kicked himself free from Jack. But instantly they were at him again like a pair of wolves.

Jim side-stepped, caught Jack by the wrist and
gave him a sharp jerk, at the same time kicking his
ankle. The fellow dropped. Whirling, the tall

woodsman with a lunge and a swing of his right
fist caught Pete on the point of the jaw, lifting him
from his feet and sending him crashing back against
the wall, where he fell and remained lying still.
Scarcely had he time to meet the renewed attack of
the other, who had arisen and flung himself at Flanagan. But with only one man to deal with Jim felt
that the tide of battle was already receding. When
Jack's arms locked round his, Flanagan slid his
hands up the fellow's back, brought them forward
past his ears and buried a long finger in each of his
assailant's eyes, forcing back his head. With an
agonied groan Jack flailed at Snohomish Jim with
his fists, but the pressure on his eyes was relentless.
Suddenly Flanagan tore the man loose, seized him,
swung him off the floor above his head and hurled
him down upon the floor.

"I think you'll sleep awhile," Jim said, breathing
heavily.

Jack slept. Likewise, Pete. Cocking his ear to
listen to the uproar in the hallway, where most of
the denizens of the hotel had been drawn by the
earthquake within, Jim glowered at the door on
which some one was pounding vigorously, and demanded:

"What's ailing you?"

At his question a silence akin to that in the room
succeeded the noise without.

"Who are you killing?" the proprietor's voice
raged. "I'll have the whole bunch of you drunks
pulled."

With a quick step Jim reached the door, which he unlocked and jerked open.

"You'll do what?" he roared.

For an instant the hotel-keeper and the crowd quailed before his savage aspect. A long scratch marked his cheek from eye to chin. Some of Jack's blood was upon his shirt. His figure filled the doorway and his face yet wore a murderous look.

"Well, let me in," said the proprietor, finally.

"Nobody else though—don't worry, I won't lay hands on you," said Jim, moving aside. "And I'll pay the damage. We've just had a little argument."

"Argument—Great God! Is that what you call it!" The man gasped, as advancing he caught sight of the wrecked interior and the two prostrate figures on the floor.

Flanagan closed the door to shut off the gaping crowd.

"See here, this pays," he said, stripping off some bills from the roll he produced. "Take 'em. Now, those fellers ain't as dead as they look, but maybe they're broke up some. Wouldn't be surprised if that one's jaw wasn't working, and this one here ought to have a few ribs floating loose in spots. All this came about because they didn't want to be arrested—they're a couple of dynamiters."

"Dynamiters!" the proprietor gasped anew.

"Yes—and they're going to jail. Wait till I tie 'em up, then I give you orders to call the wagon. Do you get that?"

"Damned quick. No dynamiters lodge in my hotel," was the reply of the other, whose anger had been mollified by the liberal amount of money placed in his hand.

"When the police come, tell 'em to lock these crooks up and tell 'em why," Jim continued earnestly. "For I can't stay to see to the business myself. The feller with the bombs is still ranging round— and you might say to the cops that I've gone to Stokes' shipyard. When I'm done there, I'll go to the station and give 'em the facts about these fellers. Got to get busy now."

"Shall I send the police there?"

"Yes, after they've landed these men."

Tearing a bed sheet into strips, Jim speedily bound his recent adversaries hand and foot, afterwards testing the knots and bands.

"No dynamite in here, or their rooms?" was asked him, anxiously.

"Nope. And another thing, don't talk. Haven't got all the gang yet. Tell the crowd outside it was just a row."

The proprietor nodded his understanding, but appeared uneasy.

"This is all straight, is it?" he demanded.

"Straight goods. Do I look like a crook?"

"You look like a prize-fighter, anyway."

Jim smiled grimly.

"It was coming to them," said he.

And he went out, elbowing his way through the crowd outside, and descended into the office below. There the clock showed fifteen minutes after eight.

Jim thought that he been slightly longer in argument than that. He hastily washed his hands and face in the washroom, helped himself to a handful of cigars from the cigar-case, tossed a half-dollar on its top, lighted a weed, and departed.

XXIV

THE ENEMY WITHIN OUR GATES

ELLEN DURAND had a piece of fancy-work on her lap, but the needles and thread were idle in her fingers. Her thoughts were absorbed in recollection of the words, look, touch of Robert Stokes' hand in the office that afternoon. With a queer feeling of panic, and of eagerness, she remembered them all. Ever since, she had experienced a strange tremor of heart like nothing she had ever known, that made her fearful at she knew not what. It was as if she were undergoing a change utterly new and unnamable which threatened while it exalted.

A call from the hall stair informed her she was wanted at the telephone. Aroused from her reverie, she laid aside her needles and lace and went down. Perhaps the call was from—him! But such did not prove to be the case; after she had spoken twice without reply, a strained voice came over the wire.

"Is this Miss . . . Durand?" it asked, with evident effort.

While the tone had a puzzling familiarity, the girl could not place the speaker. She could scarcely distinguish the words uttered as they apparently were in a low, labored murmur.

"Yes, this is Miss Durand? Who is speaking? What do you wish?" she inquired.

After a pause the voice made response.

"Listen. . . . Get Stokes. I've tried . . . can't. Not home."

"Go on, go on—I'm listening!" Ellen Durand cried, in swift fear.

Something in the strange, faint, halting answer of the other filled her with an extraordinary alarm. And it concerned Robert Stokes.

"Listen," the voice began again. "Mocket gone . . . blow up ships. I followed . . . shot me. Warn . . . Warn, Stokes."

"Who is this speaking? Who is this speaking?" the girl asked, in a mist of terror.

"Andrews. I tried to stop . . . him. Get Stokes . . . get . . . Stokes and men . . . yard."

"Quick! Where are you?" she cried.

"Securities Build . . . Main killed. Send doctor . . . after . . . afterwards, but warn . . . first. And stop Mocket . . . bombs, and all that . . . German . . . I'm . . . I'm all . . . in."

A rattle of the receiver falling at the other end and no further reply to her frantic appeals carried its own story. She rang up central, all at once collected of mind, determined, aroused in spirit. To the operator she swiftly announced the fact of the shooting in the Securities Building and urged that a doctor be immediately dispatched thither. Then she demanded Stokes' house telephone number and on receiving the connection learned that Robert

Stokes had left the dwelling some time before in a motor-boat for the shipyard, where he had gone to finish work in the office.

Ellen Durand ran out of the boarding-house. The fog rendered the night black and the street lights shone through it like muffled moons. The quiet of the neighborhood seemed uncanny in contrast to the clamor in her mind. A terror possessed her lest she be too late. She sped across the street and burst into a house whose owner she knew possessed an automobile.

The man and his wife sat reading, but started up at her entrance. A little girl ran into the room in wonderment.

"I work at the Stokes shipyards, and I've just learned the ships are to be blown up," she said earnestly. "Won't you take me there in your machine so I can warn Mr. Stokes and the guards. One of our clerks has just been shot, perhaps killed by the plotters."

"What!" the man exclaimed.

"Yes. And the plotters may this minute be at work to destroy the vessels. We must hurry! They shot Mr. Main too, killed him!"

" 'Gas' Main—I can't believe it!" Then with a quick leap for the door, and, "Wait for me in front!" he was gone.

Ellen Durand accompanied by the man's wife and child went out upon the veranda. To the girl the minutes seemed to fly while she awaited the coming of the car. She peered into the foggy night, heark-

ening with a pounding heart for the distant roar she
dreaded, answering vaguely the questions of the
terrified woman at her side, and clenched and re-
clenched her hands at the thought Robert Stokes
was at the shipyard and in danger.

A thrill of fear shot through her bosom. Even
now he might be seated in the office, a possible victim of the conspirators' bombs. The villains would
stop at nothing. They had shot Mr. Main—why,
she knew not. They had wounded Andrews, whom
she had believed one of them. And all the while
the silent Mocket had been the traitor, the manipu-
lator of company troubles, the scoundrel planning
the destruction of the boats and conniver with the
German agents, potential murderer. He would not
hesitate to kill Robert Stokes, if necessary to his
ends. Oh, if that happened—if Bob Stokes were
killed—— She dropped her face into her hands
and began to cry softly.

With a reckless rush the automobile shot out along
the driveway, its headlights glowing in the fog like
huge eyes. Ellen Durand ran down the steps of the
house and out to the curb, where the car throbbing
and trembling under its power came to rest. The
man motioned her to a seat by his side.

"Don't go yourselves where the dynamite is," the
anxious wife called after them.

"Um-umph," came from the man's lips, non-committally.

Away sped the car, the street a glister of moisture
before the lamps, occasionally passing the blurred

glare of an automobile headed in the opposite direction. Whirling presently into a broader avenue, the man increased the car's speed until they were racing through the muggy night in a way to satisfy even Ellen Durand's desperate mood. Once the man spoke to her, saying they had overlooked a bet, that they should first have notified the police. She answered yes. That had escaped her mind altogether; and her mind was harried by the thought that this oversight might be responsible for Robert Stokes' death. The police could have reached the shipyard much sooner than they.

At a reduced rate the car proceeded along the main business street, though nevertheless swiftly. The driver suddenly swerved alongside the curb and shouted to a policeman.

"Dynamiters at Stokes' shipyard! Turn in a call—I'm J. F. Austin, of Austin Hardware Company," he said to the officer, in short sharp tones. "There's an attempt to blow up their ships. I'm heading down there. It may happen any instant!"

Without halting for response he wheeled the car away from the spot, dodged a street car and drove on. Before the Securities Building a crowd was gathered, thronging the pavement about the entrance. It had scented that something extraordinary had occurred. Lights were hazily visible part way up the edifice.

"Was that where Main was shot? His offices are there," the man said.

"Yes," she replied. "Oh, do hurry!"

Ellen Durand's voice but expressed the fever of her soul. It seemed to her that she was burning. It seemed to her that they would never reach the shipyard, speeding toward it though they were. Only when the car swept into the street leading to the piers did she grip her palms with new hope. She sat leaning forward, her figure taut, gazing through the blurred windshield.

"When we get to the tracks, show me the way to their gate—I don't know it," the man said.

She pointed the direction. Over the rails they passed, turning into a roadway. She saw the arc-lamps strung about the yard for night protection, glowing in the mist. A switch engine with a string of cars once threatened to block their passage, but her companion pushed the automobile across in front of the train at the risk of their lives, while a wild shriek sounded from the engine's whistle. That was the last railroad track to be traversed. They dashed ahead for the gate.

Before it the car came to a stop. Leaping out Ellen Durand ran where the gate guard peered through the crack made by the partial opening of the two doors to examine the visitors.

"Johnson—you're Johnson, aren't you? I'm Ellen Durand, the stenographer; let me in!" she cried.

He opened the gate somewhat doubtfully.

"I recognize you, but no one's supposed to come in at night without an order," said he.

"I must come in, I will come in! The yard's in

danger! Enemies are planning to destroy the ships
—you must give warning!"

Before the amazed guard could detain her she
suddenly slipped through the opening and sped towards the office. The door was ajar. Throwing it
open she sprang into the building and darted towards the inner office, where a light burned. Expecting to see Robert Stokes seated at his desk at
work, indeed, with her lips framed to utter an alarm,
she halted abruptly at perceiving him absent, the
words checked in her mouth.

She stood breathing fast, minded to run forth
and question Johnson concerning Bob's whereabouts. Then she heard some one moving in the
warehouse. She hastened to the door at the opposite side of the room leading into it and usually
kept locked. But it now opened under her hand.

A single incandescent lamp burned in the middle
of the long structure, showing a number of nail-
kegs and boxes in the circle of its illumination, but
the rest of the space was concealed in shadow. A
singular quiet now pervaded the spot. The footsteps she heard had ceased. One of the wide outside
doors was open, the one fronting the east.

As her eyes became accustomed to the dim light
of the place, she saw Robert Stokes standing perfectly motionless, gazing out of the door. He remained some feet back from it in an attitude of
fixity and apparently had not heard her enter.

Hastening forward, she was about to pour forth
her warning when something in the peculiar, savage

expression of his face caused her to stop as she reached his side. A swift sidewise glance showed that he now knew she was there. His face went suddenly pale; a groan came from between his teeth.

"Don't move, either of you," a voice commanded from just outside the open door.

With a start, Ellen Durand looked thither. Vaguely outlined against the night where the dim radiance fell on the fog were the head and shoulders of a man, his breast just level with the warehouse floor. Robert Stokes' hand reached and took hers in its protecting grip. With a slow horror sickening her soul she divined the thing the man held uplifted by his head, ready to fling, and recognized the man himself—the murderer, Mocket!

* * * * * * *

Snohomish Jim had proceeded from the hotel direct to the northeast corner of the shipyard, the place appointed for a meeting by the sender of the money and the instructions. The night could not have been better suited for the nefarious purpose the conspirators had in view, what with the fog that thickened the darkness. Despite the lights in the shipyard the enclosure would be obscured and for the most part buried in gloom. Even about the building vessels where the arc lamps were numerous the mist would intensify the shadows. Unless a man were immediately within the circle of a lamp's foggy illumination, he would be but dimly seen. And realizing that the plotters were practically certain to be able to evade the yard guards, Jim Flanagan advanced with a determination to prevent at all costs the treacherous destruction of the boats.

Ten minutes' walk brought him to the railroad tracks. He crossed them on the street leading to the eastern pier, but just before arriving at the latter turned aside. A hundred feet or so of ground had to be crossed to gain the shipyard fence, a dark stretch over which he advanced carefully, feeling his way to avoid stumbles or noise. Presently he came to the fence, as he judged not far from the corner.

He gave two low whistles, the signal prescribed in the note accompanying the currency. A single word, "Here," answered him from a point a few paces off in the darkness. Towards it he walked, until he distinguished a blur he knew to be men.

"Who is it?" asked the same voice, the voice of the man who had met Pete in conference in the empty house in the outskirts of the city.

"I'm Pete's brother that he told you about," Jim responded, in a guarded tone.

"Well, the others haven't arrived yet."

"And won't, unless they sober up mighty fast," Flanagan remarked, with emphasis. "Couldn't keep 'em away from the bottle. I argued and begged, but they were started on the booze and nothing would make 'em stop. Said they had the money, so didn't need to come." Something like curses from more than one pair of lips showed Jim he was correct in his surmise that there were two or more men here.

"You're on hand, at least," the spokesman stated.

"Yes. When I'm paid to do a job, I don't lay down on it. A feller ought to get something in return for his good money. And I don't let liquor interfere with business."

A silence ensued, then the others consulted together in whispers. To Snohomish Jim it sounded as if they were exchanging views in a foreign tongue, some "wop" language.

"The night's favorable; perhaps you can do all the work yourself," was addressed to him.

The words were tentative, almost a question.

"Sure, I can," said he. "Nobody can see a feller much in this fog. What's the scheme?"

The spokesman came closer.

"We have here in a suitcase six bombs," said he, in slow, careful explanation. "With one of them I'll blow up the office building. That will bring all the guards on the run, and in the confusion and after giving them two or three minutes in which to reach the spot you'll circle round and throw the rest under the ships. You'll take the nearer vessel first and use three bombs, one each under the bow and the stern and one in the middle. Then you'll hasten to the newer boat and destroy it with the remaining two charges. There's enough high explosive in the bombs to wreck the hulls completely if you throw them as I instruct. And there will be a hundred dollars more for you when you've finished."

"Where'll I get it? You won't be hanging round long after the music starts," Jim said. "And it's a sure thing I won't be loitering none after I'm done."

"We'll wait here until you return. We want to make quite sure the ships are blown to pieces."

In the woodsman's mind there was a strong skepticism as to the conspirators lingering to pay him an extra bonus, but he did not express it.

"Have you planned our get-away?" he inquired.

"We'll escape from the yard in the same manner we enter—through two boards here at my back which we've removed from the fence. I loosened them a week ago, in such a way as not to be observed."

"And after we get outside?" Jim queried.

"You'll then have to look after yourself. We'll give you the extra hundred and you can disappear. Don't expect help from us after that. We depart by a motor-boat lying at the pier yonder and you need not think to see us again or to receive further aid. You'll have to make the best of your chances, just as we do. Now, you understand thoroughly what you have to do?"

"Absolutely understand, absolutely."

"Well, I want no mistakes, or bad work," the spokesman said.

"Leave it to me; I always give satisfaction," Jim replied. "I can hit a tree fifty yards off and these boats are considerable bigger than a tree. Can't miss 'em."

Again the plotters consulted together, while Jim stood by attempting to divine their whispers. Meanwhile he chewed tobacco with deliberate workings of his jaws.

"Come along with us," the man directed him, presently. "Follow me through the hole."

As bade, Snohomish Jim found and inserted his long body through the opening made in the fence by the removel of the boards, crowding after the leader. Behind him came the other two of the party, one uttering a word of caution in English concerning proper handling of the suitcase.

The lights of the yard were now visible. The four men advanced in silence, their figures dimly outlined to each other, passed along in the gloom of several piles of timbers and finally halted when the leader gave a low word of warning. They were in the open. The office building which stood some two hundred feet from the spot where they had entered was now but twenty paces before them. A light burned in the north end where the offices were located, but the warehouse part of the structure was a dark blur.

"I'll take one bomb," the leader told Flanagan, "then you go off yonder with the rest in the suitcase and wait, as I explained. Carry the case carefully —and wait till the guards have come in this direction before beginning work."

The speaker took the case from the man who carried it, laid it flat on the ground and after opening it removed one of the objects it contained. Then he

closed the suitcase once more and set it up straight.
Jim had sought to distinguish the features of his
three companions, but beyond seeing that the leader
was tall and thin, and the others not so tall but
stouter, he learned nothing except that one appeared
to wear a beard.

"Better let me dynamite that building, 'long with
the rest," Jim suggested.

"No," said the man with the bomb, sharply. "I
want to do that with my own hand; I want to leave
my mark on the cursed place. And besides, by
drawing the guards off the vessels, it gives you opportunity to do your own part successfully. You,
Hoffner and Herr Van Greiz, remain here till I
return."

At the names Jim glanced at the men designated.
Like a flash, his brain grasped the significance of the
plot. These were German enemies! Not only was
Stokes Brothers' property at stake, but the interests
of America as well!

He shot out a hand—it was time to act! His
fingers closed around the leader's wrist.

"Give me that bomb, you dirty traitor, or I'll blow
you all up," he growled. "I've got your number,
you Dutch hellhounds!"

All at once a heavy cane in the hand of one of the
other men rose and fell on Flanagan's head. Without a sound he went down full length. The men
bent over him, exchanging a few hurried words.
Then the leader moved away towards the ware-

house, where he slid open a door which he had provisionally left unlocked.

Back on the ground Snohomish Jim, amid a galaxy of stars, opened his eyes. A fierce throb beat on the top of his skull—but on occasion he had been hit much harder with a peavey handle. His head was tough. He gazed upward and about. In front of him with their backs his way stood two of the men. He noiselessly sat up with renewed interest. The suitcase was on the ground within reach. Getting to his feet like a shadow, he glared at the two figures. Against the glow he perceived that one leaned on a cane—if he had been sure they did not carry revolvers, he would have begun an "argument."

Presently one of the two men turned to look at their victim. He next bent over and stared, then clutched the other's arm.

"Mein Gott!" he cried. "Look!"

The prostrate figure and the suitcase both had evaporated.

XXV

A DEATH BLAST

AT the sound of one of the warehouse doors being opened which came to him faintly in the office, Robert Stokes had stopped work to investigate. Unlocking the door leading into the long dark building, he had struck a match and advanced towards the middle of the room where he snapped on a suspended electric light. Apparently the man outside had observed him come through the illuminated office door, recognizing him and watching his movements with a sardonic interest, for when Bob took a step towards the outer opening he beheld his book-keeper just outside. The bomb in the man's hand, the malevolence on his face, announced more clearly than words his infamous purpose. And Stokes realized that the conspirators had chosen this night for the execution of their plot.

But Bob remained cool.

"So you're responsible for all our troubles," he said in a low voice, playing for time. "Where's your master, Main? I'll venture to say he's keeping safe away."

Mocket's eye-glasses seemed to glitter against the dim light.

"Main's dead—and your clerk Andrews, who followed me to Main's office trying to trap me, is dead also," was the answer, given with cold insolence. "I shot them both. Main was no master of mine. And you'll have to go over the road with them, since you've stumbled in here. You'll sail up with the building and with your ships."

"Then you're the leader in this German plot to destroy our ships," Bob replied, still seeking to gain some advantage by delay. "You take our money, but sell us out and sell out your country for thirty pieces of silver, like Judas."

"My country! This land full of men seeking to wallow in money, a land too foul with the off scourings of Europe and the collected scum of the earth, isn't my country, you fool! I despise it, I spit on it! If I could take it in my hands, I would wring it till it suffered the pain I have suffered and would rend it to pieces."

"Yet it gave you welcome when you came to it," Stokes said. "It gave you employment, gave you clothes for your body, gave you food for your mouth, gave you shelter. Are you such an ingrate that you now strive to return harm for good?"

A bitter laugh was the man's answer.

"I hate it, I tell you," Mocket exclaimed, in a low fierce voice. "Every minute I have been here has been an eternity, and instead of receiving kindness I've had to crawl and lick the hands of men that were no better than I—yourself among them. I had to do that, I, in whose veins runs the blood of a

noble family. Faugh! It sickens me to think of it.
And I shall make as many of you pay for it as I
can reach!"

"So you still love Germany. For you're a German, aren't you?"

"A German, yes, the only decent race on earth.
All others are fools and shall go down in the dust.
As you shall go down!"

"And you have no doubts about your superiority,
I suppose."

A sneer sufficed to express Mocket's opinion of
that. The man continued to stand unspeaking. In
his hand he held the bomb uplifted, while his whole
attitude was one of rigid pitilessness.

Suddenly Bob heard light footsteps coming towards him across the warehouse floor, but he did
not remove his eyes from the instrument of death
which Mocket carried. But finally when he sensed
someone stood beside him, he shot a glance about
towards the person and to his horror beheld Ellen
Durand. With a feeling of despair he caught her
hand. How had she come here? What fate had led
her into this dreadful situation? Hard upon the
quick fear he had, there came a tremendous surge
of passion that cleared his brain and steeled his body
to save her life.

"Let her go safe, anyway," he demanded of the
fanatic before him in the doorway.

"To give warning to your guards? No."

Bob slipped a protecting arm about her form.

"Surely you're not cruel enough to destroy her,"

he pleaded. "She's but a girl; make your war on men if war you must make."

"Too late; she has no business here. Chance brought her here and she must therefore pay the toll. Lives shall not stand in my road to-night— your life, her life, or other lives! Main has been swept aside, Andrews swept aside; so must you be. I serve Germany!"

Stokes for all his apparent attention to the effort to persuade the murderer to leniency had been planning. Possibilities, chances, the elements of the situation, all were being swiftly calculated in his mind. The explosive force of a bomb carrying the constituents that this held by Mocket must have would be appalling. The thing would unquestionably wreck that part of the warehouse where he and Ellen Durand stood—but what of Mocket himself?

From this place to the door leading into the office was some fifty feet, and from that door through the two offices to the outside was another fifty feet; a hundred feet in all. If he snatched up Ellen and ran he should be able to cover it in ten seconds at most. Keyed to the highest nervous pitch as he was, he felt himself capable of any effort of strength and agility, anything—because he must! And unless Mocket were wholly insane, a madman, ready to immolate himself as well as others in his savage desire for revenge and punishment, he himself should have to retreat at least fifty feet from the building to escape the effect of the explosion.

"Well, if that thing in your hand is the real article you'll be blown to pieces along with us," Stokes remarked.

"Your solicitude is interesting," came the other's mocking answer. "But you may be sure that I shall take good care of my own skin. I have a great deal to do before I cease operations, my dear employer. For one thing, I want to see your ships go up in kindling wood; two friends are ready and merely waiting to hear my shot, which is their signal. You would have been in hades by now had I not seen your light through this open door and decided to see who I was to send into eternity. It rather pleases me it is a member of the firm; that gives distinction to the affair."

Stokes felt Ellen Durand's fingers grip his arm in terror.

"You imagine you can stand there and throw the bomb without receiving injury?" Bob asked skeptically.

"Oh, I shall retire a suitable distance."

Bob's arm tightened about the girl and his whole body tensed as he realized the instant for action was at hand.

"But how about those guards there behind you?" he questioned, in a voice of exaggerated contempt. "See them?"

Mocket whirled about, crouching in alarm, peering this way and that at the darkness with his near-sighted eyes. Look as he would, he saw no one; he again glanced about on all sides to make certain;

then he realized that he had been duped by the oldest of tricks. Turning angrily around he cried:

"You imbecile Yankee, I'll——"

But the doorway was empty. The long warehouse indeed no longer held the man and girl whom he had expected to sacrifice to sate his passion for destruction, in truth verging on insanity, and he beheld against the panel of light framed by the inner office doorway Stokes with Ellen Durand in his arms vanishing from view. While he had stupidly stared into the gloom for imaginary guards, the youth had lifted the girl, ran stealthily on tiptoe from the place, escaped.

Venting an oath on the doorway Mocket rushed back from the building, lifted his arm and hurled the bomb forward.

On the opposite side of the structure and from the office door at the north end Bob Stokes had staggered out and was running desperately for the yard gate. He had taken half a dozen steps when a deafening roar blasted the night and flung him with his charge forward upon the earth. His head struck the ground and he lay dazed, the ringing roar still in his ears.

When he opened his eyes again, he perceived the night illuminated by a brilliant glare. The dynamite wrecked building was burning. Next instant he became conscious that Ellen Durand sat on the ground supporting his head in her lap, bending her face over him and softly sobbing.

•

"Don't cry. I'm not dead, by a long way," he said.

At his words she quickly drew his head against her breast, where she held it close.

"I should have died too if you had been killed," she said.

"When you came into the warehouse there and stood beside me," he answered, slipping an arm upward and drawing down her face so he could kiss it, "I knew then, as if our danger had opened my eyes, that I loved you and should never let you go again. I knew too that you had seen me there threatened by that man and had come in at the risk of your life to save me. What a brave heart you have!"

"I do love you; I want to be with you always, Bob."

"And you shall, sweetheart."

Once more he kissed her damp, tear-stained face and then arose to his feet, afterwards helping her up.

"But how did you happen to be here at the yard to-night?" he questioned, earnestly.

"Mr. Andrews 'phoned me this terrible man had shot him. He had tried to warn you, but failing that called me up. And, oh, it sounded as if he were dying while he spoke! Then I rushed here in a neighbor's automobile when I was told you were at the office, and when I was inside I heard you in the warehouse, looked in, saw you about to be killed. That instant I knew you were everything to me."

.

Just then a nearby voice spoke. Stokes turning his head perceived Snohomish Jim standing an interested spectator.

"Feeling all right now, Bob? There won't be any more shootin' bombs in the yard, for I'm packin' the rest of 'em here in this suitcase. Arrived about this spot when you came tumbling out. We better go after the men; they haven't been gone but a minute. Told me they expected to beat it in a boat they had tied up at the east pier."

"I know the boat. If they get away now, there'll be no catching them at all," Bob stated, hurriedly.

"I dread to have you go!" Ellen cried.

"Come along, boy—excuse us, lady," Jim said.

"Be careful, be careful, Robert! You musn't be injured now when the danger is over," Ellen whispered, clinging to him.

"I shall catch these men if possible. The boat I came in from the house is tied at the water's edge across the yard, where I had a carpenter make an opening in the fence, a door I can lock. Come on, Jim, we'll beat them to it."

At that moment a patrol of police ran into the yard to augment the guards already protecting the ships.

"See that a fire call is put in, if the watchman hasn't already done so," Bob said to the girl. "We'll not be gone long."

Skirting piles of lumber, now rendered visible by the light of the burning warehouse, Stokes and Flanagan hastened to the fence at the eastern side of the yard, followed it along to the water, and there emerged through Bob's private gate upon the beach of the basin. A brief search found the motor-boat moored at the spot where it had been left.

"We haven't any guns," Bob exclaimed in some anxiety.

"Well, we've got something else," said Jim. "Hop in. We don't want to give those fellers any time to breathe. I reckon they haven't got to their boat yet, though doubtless they're running their legs off. They've got to go without attracting notice. It would give 'em all away, on top of the explosion if they chased too fast. Run the boat quiet, boy. We've got to listen some in this fog."

"I'll keep her close in by the pier," Stokes answered.

The boat was pushed free. In the bow Jim took up watch with the precious suitcase between his feet. From the streets before the shipyard sounded the clamor of approaching fire engines. Calls and shouts were heard about the shipping of the water-front where the roar of the bomb had stirred all hearers to excitement. Through the fog the glow of the fire in the company's enclosure illuminated the night.

Stokes and Flanagan had progressed at slow speed for a quarter of the length of the pier when they heard the sudden popping of an exhaust at their left. In the darkness they could make out nothing, but Bob kept his craft moving ahead. The direction of the sounds changed, as if the other craft had moved out from the pier and now approached nearer.

"Let her have gas; here they come, I bet a dollar!" Jim exclaimed.

Stokes had given his boat a swing away from the shipping in order to gain room and at Flanagan's utterance pressed the accelerator. Over his shoulder and against the glow of the fire behind he saw the shape of another boat containing men sweeping toward them. It was not fifty feet away. On its present course it would pass the spot farther to the west, as it appeared to be veering sharply from the pier, seeking the cover of night. Again Bob changed his direction so as to bring him nearer the other craft. That the men were not aware of a second boat running parallel with and a little in advance of their own was certain.

"I'll have to ram them, Jim," he said. "Or they'll get away."

Jim was busy with something at his feet.

"Get close and order them to stop, first," he answered.

Both boats were now traveling fast. The conspirators' purpose was plainly to escape to sea, where either some vessel awaited to pick them up or where they planned to skirt the coast until they won Mexican waters.

The blurred lights on both piers marked the harbor from which they were passing. Once the tall dim shape of a vessel with riding lights, at anchor in the basin, loomed up and fell away at one side in the darkness. At the pace the two craft were going Bob did not dare risk trying to bring his boat nearer the other except at a long angle, for fear of falling astern and losing it altogether. He was getting all out of his little scooter that he could, but the second boat, large and strongly engined, was picking him up as he could tell by the increased noise of its exhaust. The enemy was now not more than thirty feet off, and almost even; in another two minutes their boat would be in front.

"Halt, you men!" Jim shouted.

A quick exclamation of alarm came in reply, then hurried exchange of cries among the occupants of the opposite craft. A pistol flashed, flashed a second time, while the reports rang over the water.

"Steady, Bob, hold her level," said Jim.

He hurled something outward in the darkness. In short stabs their enemies' revolvers continued to flame in the blackness. Twice bullets splintered the woodwork of the hull. And the conspirators were gaining; the exhaust of their boat roared like a humming wheel in the fog.

Suddenly Bob perceived Jim rise in the bow, his figure vague and portentous. The flashes of the pistols had ceased for a moment, but now began again. The other boat was scarcely twenty feet away; its stern was even with their bow.

"Hold fast, Bob—hell may pop!"

His arm swung and hurled twice, thrice.

"Get 'em, get 'em," Stokes was grating through his teeth,

"Steady, boy, steady—this is the last! . . .
Aha!"

Their boat seemed suddenly lifted and dashed
down upon the dark waters, as a blinding flash and
roar rent the darkness of the harbor. For one instant Stokes and Flanagan seemed to see a geyser
spouting upward that bore planks and spume and
figures of men, then night clapped down again and
the pair were tossing and rocking in the fog, lying
where they had been flung flat on the bottom of their
boat, the sound of the explosion still ringing in their
ears. Where the other craft had been was—
nothing!

XXVI

THE FIRST SHIP

On the morning of July Fourth, at about the hour of eleven o'clock, most of Martinsport was gathered in the shipyard of Stokes Brothers, which was gaily decorated with flags and bunting. Frederic Stokes, freed of his plaster cast at last, was there with his wife and sitting in Mr. Willard's motor car. Beside the latter was Broussard's automobile, in which reposed Andrews, pale and weak, with a nurse at his side—his first day out of the hospital. Among the town's prominent citizens present were Derland, Johnson and Farrington. The latter pair wore the pleasant dignified manner such an important occasion merited. And there were the unnamed thousands who joined in the double holiday of the nation's anniversary and of the launching of the first vessel built in Martinsport.

The circumstances under which the ship had been built made its successful construction the more noteworthy. War had touched, though secretly, the little city. Every soul present knew of the conspiracy to wreck the vessels, though uninformed of the details, and therefore a glamor hung about the huge hull ready to slip into the sea.

All at once at a signal the blocks were knocked away. An American flag on the ship began to wave gently, the ship itself to move on the way. A cheer arose from the throng. On the deck where stood Ellen Durand, Robert Stokes and John Stokes, Flanagan and others, among them city and state officers, there was a flutter of handkerchiefs and flags. Ellen Durand bent over and swung an object attached by a cord against the side of the vessel's bow; there came a splash and gleam of shining drops in the sunlight. A band was playing, but the roar from the crowd drowned its strains. Again and again that wave of sound swept the throng.

At first traveling slowly though gathering speed as it proceeded along the greased way, the ship moved down into the sea. As it took the water a great wave of foam curled up about the stern where was painted the name—ELLEN DURAND.

Bob Stokes caught and pressed the girl's hands, smiling down at the happiness on her face. Off the wooden track and out upon the waters of the harbor slid the ship, sending an immense surge beating forth to either pier, and floated there shining bright and strong in new paint, her flag waving free to the breeze.

Snohomish Jim lifted his hat aloft with a solemn air and spoke.

"The finest ship, the finest girl, the finest flag floatin'—I salute 'em all. That's me!"

THE END

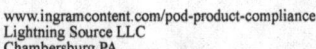

9 781479 478545